Charlie Small's
ADVENTURE DIARY

No. 2

This diary belongs to: Charlie Small

Address: Pangaean Ocean, PO6 GBH

Age: ~~Twelve~~ 400 (I must be by now!)

Mobile: Stolen by pirates!

School: I am way too old for school!!!

Things I like: Swinging through trees; chatting to gorillas; Grip and Grapple

Things I ~~h~~ ... ...he silverback (a bully) ... ...ough of them ...

Publisher's Note
This diary was found encased in a block of ice, high in the Himalayas. But what has happened to Charlie Small himself? We want to know! S... across a lost boy... ...

London Borough of Merton

M00847781

I hate deck
swabbing !!

All aboard The Betty Mae!

THE LOST DIARY OF CHARLIE SMALL VOL 2

PIRATE GALLEON

Who knows what lurks at the bottom of the ocean?

The second diary of my amazing, astonishing, INCREDIBLE ADVENTURES!

GUPPY BOOKS

THE LOST DIARIES OF CHARLIE SMALL: PIRATE GALLEON
is a GUPPY BOOK

This edition published in the UK in 2023 by
Guppy Books,
Bracken Hill,
Cotswold Road,
Oxford OX2 9JG

First published in the UK by David Fickling Books, a
division of Random House Children's Books, in 2009

Text and illustrations copyright © Nick Ward, 2009

978 1 913101 923

1 3 5 7 9 10 8 6 4 2

Papers used by Guppy Books are from well-managed
forests and other responsible sources.

GUPPY PUBLISHING LTD Reg. No. 11565833

A CIP catalogue record for this book is available from the British Library.

Typeset by Falcon Oast Graphic Art Ltd
Printed and bound in Great Britain by CPI Books Ltd

If you find this book, <u>PLEASE</u> look after it. This is the only true account of my remarkable adventures.

My name is Charlie Small and I am at least four hundred years old. But in all those long years, I have never grown up. You see something happened when I was twelve. I went on a journey... and I'm still trying to find my way home.

I narrowly escaped the clutches of a huge silverback gorilla only to find myself sailing the seas on a rotting pirate galleon! I have walked the plank and fought giant slugs, but I still look like any twelve-year-old boy you might pass in the street.

You may think this sounds fantastic, you could think it's a lie, but you would be wrong. Because <u>EVERYTHING IN THIS BOOK IS TRUE.</u> Believe this single fact and you can share the most incredible ~~my~~ journey ever experienced!

<u>Charlie Small.</u>

Caught Red-Handed

I finally escaped from Gorilla City in the dark, dense jungle, and found shelter in this fortified cabin. Now I'm in more danger than ever! I foolishly helped myself to some grub, but then fell fast asleep . . .

You can read about that in my other Journal 'Gorilla City'.

I awoke with a start when the door to the building *CRASHED* open and a band of robber pirates charged into the room! As they edged towards me, cutlasses at the ready, I could see that they were a gang of the most gruesome, ghastly and grisly bandits you could ever meet . . . and to my surprise, they were all *female* pirates!

The gang of lady pirates gathered around me. I

was sitting at their dinner table, still groggy from
having fallen into an exhausted sleep after pigging
out on their food. Horrible smiles split the pirates'
faces, exposing rows of rotting teeth. I had been
caught red-handed, and the pirates were as pleased
as punch!

'Well, what do we have here?' sneered the
captain, her gold bracelets jangling as she lifted her
cutlass to my throat.

'Uh, eh, oh!' I grunted in reply. I don't know
whether it was from sheer terror at having the
point of a huge bloodstained cutlass pressed
against my neck, or because I had spent so long

3

among the jungle gorillas, but I was finding it difficult to speak. One wrong move and I would be sliced open like a ripe peach.

'I said, *What do we have here?*' repeated the captain, giving a jab with her cutlass. 'Is it a little sand worm? A hermit crab? A skinny starfish? Well, speak up – what are you?'

Of course, they knew perfectly well what I was. They were just teasing me, making me sweat! I told them I was a boy called Charlie Small.

'A boy?' The captain scoffed. 'A sneak thief, more like! Well, we don't like boys.'

'We don't like boys,' repeated the others, grinning. 'And we don't like sneak thieves.'

'Don't like sneak thieves?' I cried, thinking of all the jewels and gold I'd seen in the next room. 'That's rich! There's a room full of stolen stuff behind that door!'

'So, you saw our special things, did you?' said the captain, with an even harder edge to her voice. 'Well, well, well. That is a shame for you, because now we can never let you go. What shall we do with him, girls?'

'Slice him!' they roared. 'Skewer him! Skin him alive!'

'Dice him, sauté him in rum and cook him over a low heat!'

'He would make a tasty starter—'

'No!' I yelled. I had to put a stop to this, before I ended up bubbling in a pot. 'I'm, er . . . tougher than you think. I would be much too chewy to eat, even stewed. If you let me live, I could be useful.'

'Useful? Useful how?'

'Well, I can cook a bit, and I could clean this place up – I could be your cabin boy!'

The captain gave me a long look.

'Lock him in the strongroom, girls,' she said. 'I've got some thinking to do.'

In The Lock up

I was thrown into the treasure room and the door slammed behind me. I could hear the bolts and padlocks clunking shut, and I knew there would be little chance of escape.

It was very gloomy inside; there were no windows in the room and the only light came from the small grille set in the door. I had no option but to wait and see what happened.

This was one of the worst situations I'd ever found myself in. Sure, I'd fought terrifying crocodiles and wrestled great apes, and even survived attacks by ravenous hyenas and massive snakes, but I'd never been locked up while my enemies discussed how to finish me off!

What were they planning? Was I going to be thrown from the cliffs onto the pointy rocks below? Or barbecued and served up as kebabs. Or— *Stop it*, I thought. I was beginning to scare myself, and I needed to be thinking of some way to escape.

I searched the room to see if there was anything that might be useful, and among a stack of dusty maps, hidden behind a mound of glittering golden goblets, I found a chart that showed the exact position of the pirates' island. They call it Perfidy, and it's a tiny dot in the middle of a huge sea called the Pangaean Ocean.

Will I end up
in a shark
infested
sea ?

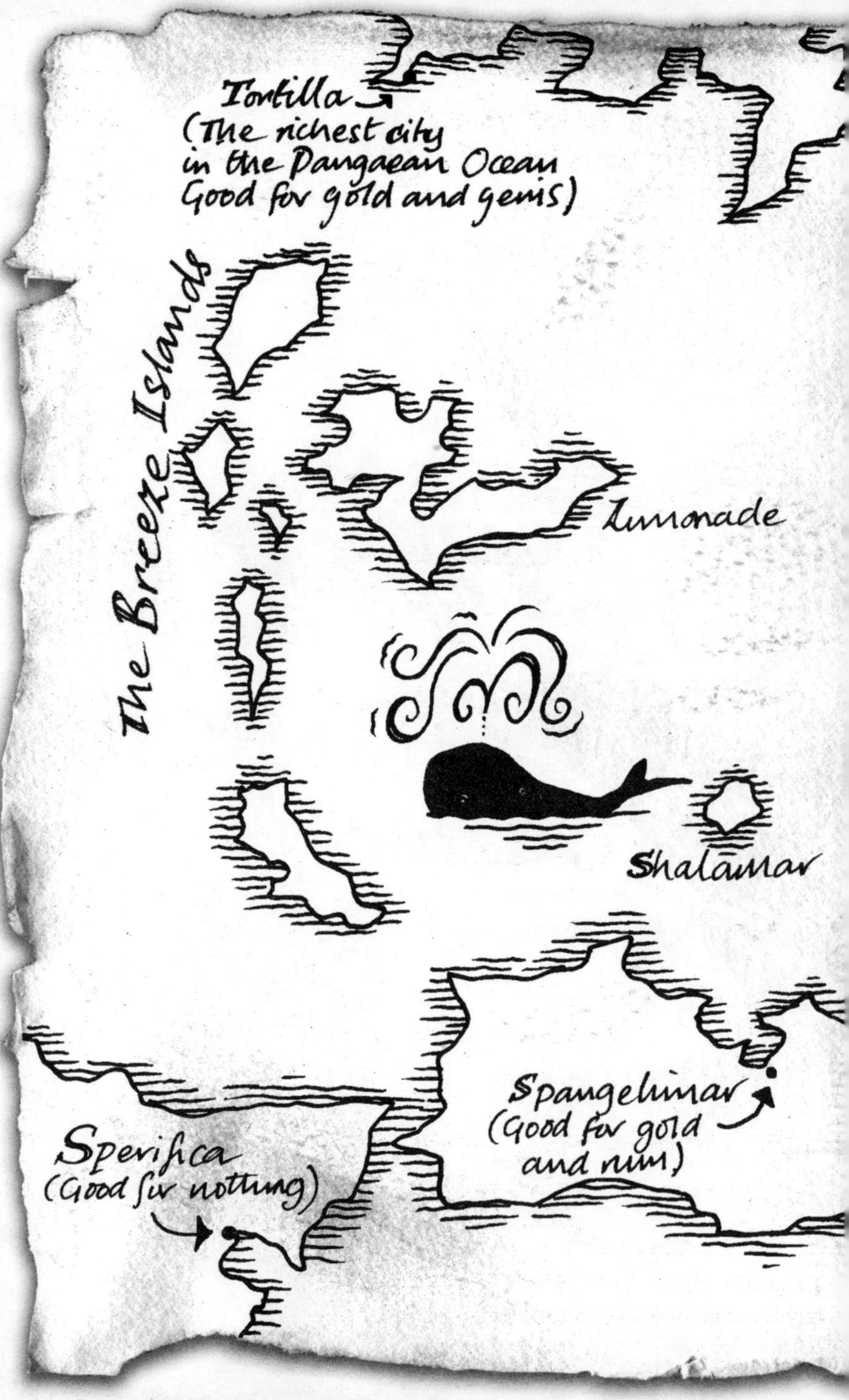

Tortilla
(The richest city
in the Pangaean Ocean
Good for gold and gems)

The Breeze Islands

Lumonade

Shalamar

Spangelimar
(Good for gold
and rum)

Sperifica
(Good for nothing)

Anyone who gives away the location of Perfidy Island will be throttled

Perfidy

Skull Island

Pangaean Ocean

N W E S

Gizzard Coast

Amonia

1000 KM

Printed by The Skeleton Press for registered pirates of the Pirate League only

Although I must have read a hundred explorer books at home, I didn't recognize any of the names on the map. But I knew it might come in useful one day, so I rolled it up and hid it inside the water bottle at the bottom of my rucksack.

As I did so, my left hand brushed against my mobile phone. My mobile! I hadn't tried to use it for ages because whenever I'd called home, Mum never listened to anything I told her. And she always replied with precisely the same words – as if it was still the same day I'd started out on my adventures and she was expecting me home for tea!

But maybe my mobile would work properly now that I was out of the jungle, I thought hopefully.

I attached my wind-up charger, spun the handle and dialled the number.

'Mum!' I cried when she answered the phone.

'Oh, hello, darling, is everything all right?'

'Well, not really! I've been captured by pirates and locked in a treasure room—'

'Sounds wonderful, dear,' Mum said. 'Oh, wait a minute, Charlie. Here's your dad just come in. Now remember, don't be late for tea . . .'

'Mum, listen,' I whispered hoarsely. She was saying exactly the same things as before. Could she hear me? I had to make her understand. 'I'm a prisoner!' I cried. 'I'm on the island of Perfidy and—'

But just then the door flew open and the captain strode into the room.

Sentence Is Passed

'Who are you talking to, boy?' she demanded, scanning the treasure room with her dark, angry eyes.

'N-no one,' I stammered, hiding the phone behind my back. But too late – the captain had already seen it.

'What have you got there? Have you been helping yourself to my precious jewels?' she growled. 'Show me at once!'

I hesitated, and she drew her cutlass and brought it crashing down on one of the packing cases with such force that it split open; a sultan's ransom worth of treasure spilled out onto the floor. 'Come on!'

Shaking, I held out the phone. Its screen glowed bright in the gloom.

'What rare jewel is this, boy?' she gasped.

'It's a phone,' I said. 'You use it to talk to people.'

The pirate captain looked confused and I realized I'd better show her before she started swinging her cutlass again!

I quickly dialled the speaking clock and handed her my mobile.

'*At the third stroke, the time will be . . .*' The captain leaped back, dropping the phone and drawing her sword.

'Who's in there?' she thundered, her cutlass hovering threateningly above the display screen. 'Come out and fight like a woman!'

I picked up the phone, trying to reassure the pirate captain that there was nothing to be frightened of.

'It's just a machine and you can talk to people

on the other side of the world with it,' I explained.

'Oh, so it's a talking machine, is it?' she said in a strangely calm voice.

I nodded, and sighed with relief that I'd made her understand.

'Do you think I'm daft, boy?' she roared suddenly. 'There's no such thing! This here is a *magic* box, a wizard's toy, and it must be worth a thousand fortunes. What's more,' she added, putting my phone and charger in her pocket, 'it's *my* magic box now!'

'No!' I cried. 'I need it.' The mobile was my only link to home, and somehow I felt sure that if I lost it, I'd never be able to get back.

'You won't need it where you're going, boy.' The captain grinned.

'What do you mean?'

'It's the drop for you,' she growled, stepping so close that her rum-soaked breath made my eyes smart.

'The drop!' I cried. 'But what about me becoming your cabin boy?'

'We don't want a cabin boy, boy. We don't want males of any description on our ship, whether they're boys, men, dogs or rats. It's a female ship and that's how it'll stay. You'll be hanged immediately from the nearest yardarm.'

What's a yardarm? I thought.

Whatever it was, hanging from it didn't sound too good.

'Follow me,' she ordered and led me out into the courtyard.

I gulped. How on earth was I going to get out of this?

The Nearest Yardarm

When my eyes had adjusted to the bright sunlight of the pirates' compound, I saw that the rest of the pirates had been busy. In the centre of the yard they had erected a ship's mast. A long rope with a noose at the end dangled from the crossbar. So that was what a yardarm was: a pirates' gallows!

I stopped in my tracks, but the captain pushed me towards the yardarm as one of her crew held the noose open, inviting me to put my head in.

'Just a minute,' I cried in a blind panic, and turned to the captain. My heart was pounding

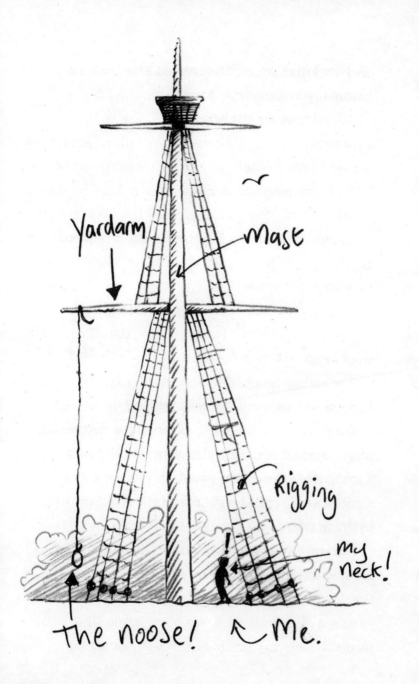

Yardarm

Mast

Rigging

my neck!

the noose! ← Me.

and my knees were knocking but I had to act now, before it was too late.

'What have we got here?' She smirked. 'A squeaker?'

'We like 'em when they squeak,' chorused the others. '*Oh mercy, oh save me!*'

But I wasn't going to beg for my life, I was going to *win* it. I was hoping that these sailors enjoyed a gamble as much as my Uncle Will, who was in the merchant navy.

'I bet I can climb to the top of the rigging before the best of your crew,' I said, praying that they would take up my challenge.

The captain rubbed her hands together. 'A wager, is it?' she said. 'What's the bet?'

I said that if I won, the captain had to return my phone and set me free right away.

'And if you lose?' she asked.

'If I lose,' I replied with a shiver, 'I'll put my head in the noose.'

'Agreed?' yelled the captain to the rest of the crew, and they roared their approval.

Me And My Big Mouth

I stood at the base of the rigging, which stretched up to the top of the mast, waiting for the pirates to choose their best climber. After years as king of the jungle, I was pretty sure that I could beat any of the pirates, no matter how long they had been climbing the rigging. Not many animals in the jungle were as quick as me at swinging through the trees; only a few of the smaller monkeys were faster.

'I'm waiting,' I said nonchalantly to the pirates as they huddled in a circle having a discussion.

'Get Bobo,' said the captain to one of her crew, who waddled off with a sailor's gait to a little shed in the corner of the yard and opened the door. A large brown streak bolted out of the shed, raced across the yard and, shrieking loudly, leaped into the captain's arms like an oversized baby.

My heart sank into my shoes. Bobo was a mandrill, just like those in the jungle, and I knew from experience how fast they could climb. A cold sweat broke out on my forehead and I felt a wave of nausea as I imagined the noose tightening around my neck. I had made a serious mistake.

'That's not fair!' I exclaimed. 'I said I would race the best of your crew. Not a monkey!'

'But Bobo is a member of the crew,' said the captain, stroking the grinning ape under the chin. 'A valued and very ruthless member.'

'Well, I still don't think it's fair,' I protested.

'You made the rules, boy, and now you must race – or hang!'

A Race To The Top

The mandrill grinned as I dumped my coat on the ground and rolled up my sleeves, her eyes fixing me with a malevolent stare.

'*Aah aah aah*,' she screamed, and raced up and down the first few metres of the rigging for practice. At a growl from the captain, we stood on either side of the mast, gripping the first rung of the rigging and waiting for the start. My heart was pounding. This really was a race for life. The captain drew her pistol, raised it in the air and fired. *BANG!*

We leaped onto the rigging, the monkey taking

an early lead; but I soon caught up as my hands and feet effortlessly found purchase in the rope netting. Bobo stared across at me in surprise. She had not expected me to be able to keep up, and she redoubled her efforts, taking the lead once more. As we raced to the top of the mast, I knew that I was going to lose. Bobo was just too fast. I had to do something quickly.

'Watch out, Bobo,' I yelled in perfect gorilla. 'Your tail is on fire!'

I knew she would be able to understand and she did. She was so surprised to hear me speak in the gorillas' tongue that she stopped and inspected her rear, before remembering that she didn't have a tail. By the time she had recovered, I had overtaken her. We both dashed for the top, Bobo screaming in indignation. But the distraction had worked and I scrambled onto the top of the mast and sat there, arms raised in victory, with Bobo less than a metre behind and shrieking like a banshee.

Before we climbed down, I offered Bobo my hand in a sporting gesture, but she was having none of it. She bared her teeth and screamed at me, 'Cheat, fraudster, conman! Where did you learn to speak gorilla?'

'Calm down, monkey,' I replied, stunned by her maliciousness. 'I used to live in the jungle. I was a gorilla king.'

But Bobo was obviously unimpressed with this bit of news. 'Well, you're king of nothing here, boy,' she said, and spat at me before scuttling down the rigging and diving once more into the arms of her beloved captain.

I followed her down, feeling very relieved. Although I'd made an enemy of one of the nastiest of animals, I had won my bet. But would the pirates keep their side of the bargain?

They were very sulky. They had been looking forward to a nice hanging, but agreed that I wouldn't swing. Not that day, anyway.

'Right, then,' I said, trying to sound more confident than I felt. 'If you'll just give me back my phone, I'll be on my way.'

'Not so fast!' roared the captain, and the pirates closed in around me. 'How do we know you haven't filched any of our precious jewels?' And before I could squirm away she ripped the rucksack from my back and upended my explorer's kit into the dirt. There was:

1) My multi-tooled penknife
2) A ball of string
3) The water bottle (with the map hidden inside!)
4) A telescope
5) A scarf
6) An old railway ticket
7) This journal
8) My pyjamas
9) A pack of wild animal collector's cards
10) A glue pen (to stick any interesting finds in my book)

Humbugs
(very strong!)

11) A big bag of Paterchak's mint humbugs (half empty)
12) The wind-up charger for my phone
13) A glass eye from the steam-powered rhinoceros
14) A huge leaf from the heart of the jungle
15) The hunting knife, the compass and the torch I'd found on the sun-bleached skeleton of a lost explorer
16) The tooth of a monstrous river crocodile
17) A slab of Kendal mint cake

'What a load of old rubbish,' sniggered one of the pirates. But it didn't stop her from pocketing the hunting knife and torch.

I crossed my fingers, hoping no one would touch the water bottle.

The captain pushed my other things around with her foot, looking disappointed. 'No sparklers, boy?' she asked me. 'No more magic boxes?'

I shook my head, hoping she wouldn't crush any of the important finds I'd saved from my adventures so far.

'Then how do you plan to pay us to take you back to the mainland?'

I blinked stupidly. I hadn't thought of that. 'Isn't there a ferry?' I asked, playing for time as I hurriedly gathered my things back into my bag.

'You're hundreds of miles from anywhere, boy. And no one knows about this island but us!' The captain leered at me. 'We're your only ticket off this island. And if you can't pay . . . you'll have to be put to work! Take him aboard the *Betty Mae*, girls, and prepare to sail!'

The 'Betty Mae'

And that's where I am now. I may not be dangling from the yardarm, but I'm more of a prisoner than ever!

I'm locked in a stunningly smelly storeroom, and I've been chained to a heavy beam. The floorboards on which I'm sitting are slippery with damp; all I can see of the outside world is a sliver of rocky headland between the rotting planks of the hull, and there's only just enough light to write by.

I have no idea what will happen to me. Will I be expected to plunder and pillage as a member of the pirates' bloodthirsty gang? I don't even know where we're sailing to. Will there be any chance of escape when we get there? And how will I get my phone and charger back from the captain?

There are so many questions that I don't know the answer to. I can hear the pirates cursing and shouting above me, and the ship creaking and groaning. I know that I'll just have to wait and see what happens.

I will continue my journal as soon as I can.

I had to put on these ←iron socks!

down with pirates

There was a decomposed jellyfish in the corner.

N
E
W
S

Which way is home?

Pirates Stink True!

A Cabin Boy's Duties!

I'll never complain about having to tidy my room
at home again. I've been working non-stop and I
am absolutely exhausted; I'm almost too tired to
feel scared, but not quite! From the moment we
reached the open sea I was put to work. And you
won't believe the chores I have to do.

This morning a wrinkly old pirate collected me
and took me up on deck, where the captain was
barking out orders and cuffing any of the crew who
didn't move fast enough.

'Ah, there you are,' the captain growled. 'Well,
you wanted to be our cabin boy, so you can start
earning your keep. Here's a list of your chores.'

She handed me a grubby cylinder of paper,
which unrolled as I took it from her. I gasped; the
list was as long as my arm! I squinted at the terrible
writing and started to read:

5.30 a.m.	Get brekfust for hole crew (200)
7.00 a.m.	Serv brekfust
8.00 a.m.	Wash up
9.00 a.m.	Scrub mayn dek

10.00 a.m.	Not good enuf. Scrub it agen
11.00 a.m.	Tea and cakes – for crew, not yew
12.00 noon	Make captins hamuck and tidee her room
1.00 p.m.	Get lunch for hole crew
2.30 p.m.	Wash up
4.00 p.m.	Repair sayels
5.00 p.m.	Cleen Bobo's cage
5.30 p.m.	Start gettin tee
7.00 p.m.	Serv tee
8.00 p.m.	Wash up
9.00 p.m.	Hav your dinna (water, bred and seegull spred only, on payn of deth)
9.10 p.m.	Lite oil lamps
9.30 p.m.	Cleen the bog
10.00 p.m.	Plump captins pillows
10.30 p.m.	Bring captins rum
11.00 p.m.	Read captins bedtime story
11.30 p.m.	Anythin els captin can fink of
Midnite	Lock up

'That's impossible,' I gasped. 'There's no way I can do all that. I can't even keep my own bedroom tidy!'

'You wanted to be cabin boy,' said the captain. 'Of course, if you can't do it, you can always go for a long walk on a very short plank . . .'

'OK, where's the kitchen?' I gulped.

'That's more like it, boy. And it's a galley, not a kitchen!'

Charlie Small, Chef!

I've never cooked a thing at home, and since I've been on my adventures I've lived mostly off bananas and Paterchak's mints. I've got no idea about proper cooking and I've never heard of half the names on the jars that lined the shelves in the galley.

When I saw the state of the sink, I groaned in horror. It was piled high with pots and pans, which had obviously not been washed for years. Dried food coated every one and furry patches of mould sprouted from the smelly, stagnant gunge that had set in the bottom of the pans and had me gasping for breath. It was disgusting. I looked around for the washing-up liquid.

Of course, there wasn't any – only a filthy scrubbing brush that looked as if it had been

used to wash coal. I gave a long groan. There was nothing for it but to roll up my sleeves and get started.

I scrubbed, I hacked and I polished for hours, until my arms ached and my hands were as wrinkled as my gran's. Eventually I had the pans lined up in a row, gleaming like new. I felt quite pleased with myself and was wondering what I could possibly cook that anyone would want to eat when the captain marched in to see how I was doing.

'Is dinner ready?' she demanded, sniffing the air expectantly.

'No, but I've finished washing the pots,' I explained, waiting for a gasp of admiration as I pointed to the rows of sparkling saucepans.

'What do you want to waste your time washing them for? We do all our cooking in that,' barked the captain, pointing to a vast pot in the corner that was big enough to stew a hippo in. 'Now get a move on, or I'll have a mutiny on my hands.'

I peered into the bottom of the huge cauldron. Oh no! The insides were encrusted with dried-on food, so I got the scrubbing brush, a hammer and a chisel, climbed inside the pot and started to scrub all over again.

It took about half an hour to shift the worst of the muck, and then I lit the fire and poured in a few buckets of water. Now what? I searched the shelves and found a recipe book called *100 Favourite Pirate Platters*. That'll do, I thought.

The book fell open at a page headed 'Wriggling Stew'. Oh, yuck! The main ingredient was eels – lots of them – but it looked quite simple to make, so I searched the galley and when I lifted the lid of a barrel, I got the fright of my life. It was alive

A slithery, slimy
Pangaean Eel (yuk!)

with fat, slippery, writhing eels. I needed fifty
of them, but when I tried to pick one up, it shot
straight out of my hands, plopped onto the floor
and wriggled out of the door, across the deck and
into the sea. This was going to be harder than I
thought!

I tried again with the same result. I needed some help, so I popped my head out of the door just as a huge, grizzled pirate walked by.

'Excuse me, but I can't get the eels out of the barrel.'

The pirate stopped and stared at me as if I was a rat's tail she had discovered in her soup. 'So?' she asked.

'Well, I'm making Wriggling Stew and it won't be very tasty without any eels, will it?' I was pretty sure it wouldn't be very tasty *with* eels, but I didn't say so.

'Wriggling Stew? That's my favourite,' The pirate beamed and pushed past me into the galley. She reached into the barrel, grabbed an eel with an iron grip, plopped it onto the table, whipped out a vicious-looking machete from her belt and . . . *Clump!* Forty-nine other eels followed it into the pot. Satisfied, the pirate wiped her hands on her trousers and left me to finish the meal.

I added all the other ingredients – onions and peppers, strange spices and herbs – and stirred and stirred while the eels' slime thickened the liquid into a stodgy stew. It actually smelled quite nice, and I was starving hungry, so I found a ladle and was just about to have a taste when there was a screech from the window. It was Bobo. She had been keeping an eye on me the whole time, and now I remembered what the captain had said. I was on prisoner rations of water and bread with seagull spread. I couldn't imagine what might happen if I was caught stealing the pirates' food . . . But I was about to find out!

Yum Yum Wriggling stew!

A Warning

The captain marched into the galley.

'So, thought you'd help yourself, did you?' she growled.

'Sorry, I forgot,' I said.

'Well, just to make sure you don't forget again, let me show you something,' she said, and I followed her out onto the deck. 'See that old cage?' she asked, pointing up into the rigging at a small, rusty pen. 'One day our last cook decided to help herself to a nice leg of pork. A whole leg, mind. But good old Bobo saw her and reported it to me. Now, the cook was quite plump and it was the devil of a job to get her into that cage. But we managed it in the end and lowered her over the side. These waters are swarming with a voracious little fish called the flesh-eating anchovy. She was only in the water two minutes, but when we hauled the cage out, it was empty, save for one bone and a slimy piece of gizzard. Do you understand, Charlie?'

The terrifying flesh-eating anchovy. (Actual size).

I understood. I wouldn't steal the pirates' food again. Or if I did, I'd make darn sure I wasn't caught!

One bone and a bit of gizzard!

The World's Number One Ladies Pirate Gang

Many days have passed, days of scrubbing and cleaning and cooking. I never get close to finishing the huge list of chores because the captain is always adding new and horrible tasks to it. And Bobo doesn't make things any easier. She does all she can to make my life unpleasant, swinging silently down from the rigging to slap me or grab my hair as she swoops past. She upsets my pail of water when I'm swabbing the decks and snitches to the captain if I miss a spot when cleaning the galley. She's just a vicious bully.

While I'm working, I try to think of ways to steal back my phone and escape, for every day brings the threat of death at the hands of the perfidious pirates. I can't trust a single one and have to be always on my guard. But even if I could get off the ship, I would still have to find dry land, and who knows how many miles away that might be? I can only hazard a guess as to where we are on the map I've hidden at the bottom of my rucksack. So, for the time being, it looks like I'm stuck on board this dilapidated barge of bad-tempered bandits. And today I learned quite a lot about them.

I was busy scrubbing the deck when I became aware that I was being watched. I looked up to find Lizzie, a large, grubby tattooed lady, leaning back against a pile of barrels with a mug of rum in one hand and a sneer on her face.

'Oh dear, you really haven't got a clue about cleaning, have you?' She smirked. 'A typical man, lazy and smelly. You're as useless as the rest of them!'

Smelly? Me? How did she have the nerve to call anyone smelly, when her pong could make a flower wilt at fifty paces? 'Oh, you'd know all about cleaning, wouldn't you,' I said sarcastically. 'I can tell by your spotless ship. I've seen cleaner dustbins!'

'We know how to scrub and clean, don't you worry,' snapped Lizzie. 'Why do you think we became pirates in the first place?'

'What do you mean?' I asked.

Lizzie poured another mug of rum, took a long glug and stared off at the horizon. 'Oh, we were all "good little housewives" once,' she said, 'keeping house for our wonderful pirate husbands while they went off for months at a time, having adventures and stealing bucketloads of dosh!'

'Your husbands are pirates?' I said.

'Oh yes – best male pirates on the Pangaean Ocean. They stole oodles of treasure. Trouble is, by the time they got home they'd spent it all. And then they had the nerve to complain if their dinners weren't waiting on the table for them when they got in. Went bonkers, they did!'

'Really?' I said, putting down my scrubbing brush and sitting back on my haunches. 'What did they do?'

'Ranted and raved and stomped and cussed. They were all the same, our husbands. They'd fly into a rage, draw their swords and storm around the house, chopping and hacking at the furniture till there was nothing left but sawdust. Then

they'd all meet down the tavern, spend the last of
their money and head back to their ship for more
adventures on the high seas. We got fed up with
it, I can tell you. We'd had enough of cleaning and
cooking while the men went off and had all the
fun. So Ivy called a meeting of all the pirate wives,
and we decided to become pirates ourselves. The
first all-lady pirate crew in the world. And we've
not done any cleaning since!'

'Who's Ivy?' I asked.

'That's the captain,' said Lizzie. 'But you
mustn't ever call her that, or she'll have your guts
for garters. She didn't think Ivy sounded scary
enough, so she changed her name to Captain
Cut-throat, and it suits her well. She's the boldest,
blood-thirstiest pirate afloat, and we've become
the scourge of the ocean.'

'Do your husbands know you've become
pirates?'

'Oh, they know all right,' chuckled Lizzie. 'One
day we attacked a big four-master. For hour after
hour our cannons roared, but when the smoke
finally cleared, we realized that the sailors clinging
to the wreckage were our husbands. Oh, how we
laughed, and oh, how they screamed: "Traitors!

Go back home and get our dinners!" Fat chance of that. Instead we took their treasure hoard, sailed to a port and shopped till we dropped. Oh, we've had some fine times,' she said dreamily.

Then she seemed to come to her senses. 'What are you sat around for, doing nothing?' she shouted. 'That's just typical of a bone-idle man.' And with that she drained her mug of rum and stomped off across the deck.

So that's why they hate doing housework so much, and why I have to work my fingers to the bone, scrubbing and polishing and tidying up their mess. I really must get off this floating prison . . . soon!

Captain Cut-throat

My Shipmates

When I first started out on my adventures, I decided to record any unusual or exotic species I might discover, and there aren't many things more unusual than this boatload of female felons. So here are a few sketches of some of my lovely shipmates:

Captain Cut-throat

The captain of the ship was called Ivy, but she didn't think it sounded scary enough, so the other pirates have to call her Captain Cut-throat. She paces the deck, shouting orders and swishing her cutlass, while Bobo follows at her heels like a large dog, sneering and screaming.

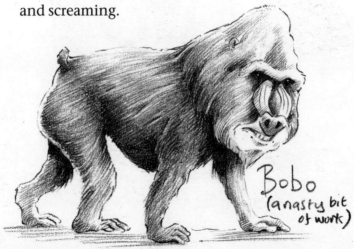

Bobo
(a nasty bit of work)

Rawcliffe Annie
Rawcliffe Annie's skin is the colour of boiled ham. She has a nose like a hatchet, which she uses to crack coconuts.

Rawcliffe Annie

Lizzie Hall

Lizzie is the pirates' champion rower. Her arms are thick with rippling muscles and she is covered with tattoos of galleons and wild animals.

Lizzie Hall has got incredible muscles!

Mop-head Kate

Kate is the youngest of the pirates, not much older than I was when I started out on my adventures. She was kidnapped during a midnight raid on a fishing village: the pirates needed a skivvy. She isn't treated much better than I am, but doesn't seem to be any friendlier than the rest of the crew.

Mop-Headed Kate was stolen from her home when she was a toddler!

Ship Ahoy!

We've been at sea for a month and the *Betty Mae* has made her first attack!

I was busy preparing a breakfast of toasted sea-sponge with a weird kind of jam called mermalaid when a cry floated down from the crow's-nest.

'*Ship ahoy, and it's a fat one!*'

Immediately Captain Cut-throat swung the ship about, and we raced after a large merchant vessel. By the time they realized they were being hunted, it was all too late.

The *Betty Mae* might be old, but she is very fast, and as Cut-throat raised the Jolly Roger, we were already alongside our prey. A cannon exploded: the *Betty Mae* was firing a warning shot across the merchantman's bows; when she heaved to, Cut-throat's crew swarmed aboard, swords at the ready and daggers clamped between their teeth.

Hiding in the shadow of our poop deck, I watched in amazement as the pirates lined up the passengers and stripped them of their jewellery, purses and long silk handkerchiefs. My heart thumped against my chest like a piston engine, but I couldn't make out whether I was scared or excited.

Some of the pirates clattered down the steps into the hold, returning with crates and boxes bulging with gold, which they brought aboard the *Betty Mae*. It was all over in a matter of minutes. No one had been hurt and I thought that maybe my pirate captors weren't so bad after all. But then I learned just how ruthless they could be.

A Long Walk

One of the passengers on board the merchant ship refused to empty his pockets.

'Clear off, you vagabonds!' he cried. 'You're not having any of my money.'

'Oh, is that so?' Captain Cut-throat smiled. 'Well, perhaps you would like some of mine . . .'

'I – I don't know what you mean,' stammered the man.

'Here, take these,' said Cut-throat, handing him two heavy bags full of gold. 'There you go. Now put them in your pockets. Go on. They're yours!'

Confused, the man put them into the deep pockets of his many-buttoned coat. His knees buckled slightly under the weight.

'Now,' said Cut-throat, 'let's go for a nice walk.' And with her cutlass she prodded the hapless man towards the ship's rails. Rawcliffe Annie appeared with a long plank of wood, and she rushed over to a gate in the rails and hammered the plank firmly to the deck, so that it stuck out over the sea.

The Unfortunate Merchant.

'I, um, I've changed my mind,' said the man when he saw the plank stretching out over the waves. 'Here – have your money back. And mine – all of it. I've got loads.'

'Leave it where it is,' warned Cut-throat. 'Now, turn round and get moving.' And she jabbed the man with the point of her sword, sending him scurrying along the plank.

the plank

Annie nailed a plank to the deck!

'Thief-taker Craik will hear of this,' the man warned.

'That old fraud!' laughed Cut-throat. 'He's nothing but a windbag. And if anyone sees him, they can tell him I said so. Now move.'

I was shocked. I couldn't believe it. Surely the captain wasn't being serious. But before I could cry out she gave a final jab with her cutlass and sent the poor man off the end of the plank. He dropped into the water and, with the weight of all the gold in his pockets, sank like a stone.

The pirates roared with delight as the man disappeared below the waves. I stood rooted to the spot, horrified by what I had witnessed, but the pirates didn't seem bothered at all. Once the man had gone, they didn't give him a second thought.

I scanned the sea for any sign of the victim. Nothing. I ran to the far side of the *Betty Mae* and looked there. Nothing. Then, all of a sudden, with a great gasp, the man bobbed to the surface. He had managed to unbutton and slip out of his coat. He was safe for the moment, but had nowhere to go.

Quickly I looked around the deck. By the mainmast I spied a stack of empty rum casks. The pirates were all too busy aboard the captured vessel to notice me, so I rushed over and heaved one into the water below. The cask floated over to the man, who heaved himself aboard and, with a silent wave of thanks, drifted away.

What a terrible bunch of scoundrels I have for shipmates, I thought. When will I be able to get away from these dangerous villains?

Story Time

Captain Cut-throat was in high spirits when I read her bedtime story that evening. She has a large stack of stolen books, but until I came along there was no one who knew how to read them! Now she insists that I read her all the adventure tales of derring-do on the high seas.

I usually look forward to the captain's story time: she's much less scary when she's roaring warnings to the hero and swinging her sword above her head. But now that I had seen what she was really like, I was in shock, and I sat beside her hammock, reading the story in a small, nervous whisper.

'Come on, Charlie, give it some feeling,' demanded Cut-throat. 'What's wrong with you tonight? Liven it up or you'll follow that old fool off the end of the plank.'

I gulped! I knew she meant it, so I swallowed

Captain Cutthroat
would wave her sword
over her head!

hard, took a swig of pirates' courage and launched
into the story anew. I put everything into it, doing
all the voices and acting out the action scenes,
leaping from chair to table to chandelier in a
desperate sword-fight with the invisible enemy.

Cut-throat loved it! She roared her approval and
spun her sword in pleasure. 'Well done, Charlie,'

she cheered at the end of the story. 'That was the best tale yet and you deserve a reward for your telling of it. What would you like, eh?'

I didn't need to think twice.

'My phone,' I said. 'I would like my phone back.'

'Oh, Charlie,' she sighed, taking my phone and charger out from underneath her pillow and stroking the phone against the side of her face. 'You know that's not going to happen. This is my most precious jewel. I'll have to think of another prize. Now, make this work!' And she handed me the mobile.

So I charged it up and went through all the ring-tones before Captain Cut-throat asked to hear the time. Then I rang the speaking clock and she held it up to her ear and grinned with delight as the recording told her it was 1.45 and 15 seconds on Sunday the 17th of April. This must have been the moment I had sailed through the tunnel of trees and my adventures began. It repeated this same information every time we phoned, but Captain Cut-throat didn't seem to mind: she sat up in bed with a look of awe on her face.

'Now, we must think about your reward,' she said, putting the phone and charger back under her pillow. 'Let me think . . . Oh, I know, food! All boys like food. How about that, eh?'

'Oh yes!' I cried, imagining myself sitting with the crew, eating my fill of roasted albatross and seaweed sauce, or shark burgers and chips. 'That would be great!'

'Good,' said Cut-throat. 'I'll get Mop-head Kate to bring you some leftovers every night. Now off to bed with you!'

Leftovers! Was that all? Well, it was better than nothing, I suppose, and after weeks of bread and seagull spread, anything will seem like a treat. So I'm back in my stinky hold, chained up and waiting to see if Mop-head will turn up with my grub. I'm not expecting a feast, but my tummy has been rumbling ever since I came on board ship, and if I'm not thinking about ways to escape or stealing back my phone, I'm usually picturing tables laden with fantastic fodder. I even dream about food at night! My tummy gurgled expectantly when I heard the key turn in the lock, and Kate came in with my reward.

Thanks A Bunch!

I stared at the bowl of gristle and wobbly, grey
tubey bits in disbelief. I was expecting at least a
slice of squid pie or a bowl of jellyfish jelly.

'Is that it?' I asked. 'Is
that my treat?'

'The captain said
to bring something
from the scraps
cupboard,' said
Kate. 'Don't you want

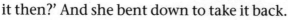

it then?' And she bent down to take it back.

'No, it's OK!' I said, grabbing hold of the bowl.
I was so hungry I could have eaten the spoon, and
I hunched over the bowl and sucked up a long,
slippery tube into my mouth. It was disgusting!

'Enjoy,'
said Kate, and
she left me
gnawing on a
lump of gristle
and a crust of
furry bread.

My floppy, tubey
dinner – yuk!

Slugging It Out

The excitement and danger never end. Today we nearly all perished when the *Betty Mae* came under a dawn attack, and it wasn't any sort of ship that nearly finished us off.

I had just been released from my lockup and had made my bleary-eyed way to the galley to prepare breakfast when, all of a sudden, the *Betty Mae* tilted at an alarming angle. Boxes and packages flew off the shelves and coals from the fire spilled dangerously across the floor. I was sent careering across the galley, but as I picked myself up, the ship tilted the other way with a cacophony of groans and squeals. Water poured across the galley floor, extinguishing the spilled coals. Then the ship lifted her nose out of the water, her stern forced down into the sea. What was going on?

I rushed outside and was met by a terrifying sight. There, lying half across the poop deck, was an enormous, disgusting slug. A giant slug. A slug as big as a house. And it was crawling out of the sea and onto our boat! As it slowly heaved itself along the deck, it dripped great gloops of gunge from its slimy body.

A giant sea slug!

Captain Cut-throat was yelling orders to her panicking crew. 'Forward, you cowardy custards!' she yelled. 'Drive it back into the sea.'

But the hapless pirates were getting caught in the slug's gunk, and stuck there as surely as if they had stepped in a puddle of glue. They yelled in terror as the slug edged forward; soon they were crushed under its huge body. The monster dipped its head, opened its great toothless, dripping jaws and . . . Well, I don't need to say what happened next.

'We're done for!' shouted Rawcliffe Annie above the cries of the other pirates super-glued to the deck.

Again the *Betty Mae* creaked and groaned, leaning dangerously as the slug continued its slow journey, and we all tumbled to the floor. Then a great dollop of slime splattered onto the deck, missing us by inches.

Some of the pirates tried to launch a lifeboat, but in their haste they tangled the ropes and it went crashing into the waves below, breaking its back as it hit the water. The mizzenmast followed, collapsing into the sea: the slug had snapped it as easily as a piece of matchwood, dripping a great pool of slime from the poop deck onto the main deck below. I had to do something, and quickly. But what? *Think, Charlie, think!* I said to myself. And then I remembered my wild animal collector's cards. I grabbed them from my rucksack and flicked through. It was a long shot, but who knows . . .? And yes, there it was: a card for the Giant Sea Slug! This is what it said:

Overall length: 20 metres

PREDATOR RATING 15

THE GIANT SEA SLUG

Beware! These huge creatures are extremely dangerous. They inhabit the depths of remote seas and capture their prey in the sticky slime that oozes from their skin. The only weapon that is effective against this grotesque creature is curry powder! (Not many people know this, or if they do, they rarely have curry powder on them when they are attacked.) Best means of defence: RUN!

WILD ANIMAL COLLECTORS CARDS

Curry powder? I groaned. Who's going to have curry powder handy when a sea slug attacks? And then I remembered – *I* did! Or chilli powder, which was the same sort of thing. At least I hoped it was.

I dashed back to the galley and searched through the casks of spices and condiments until I found the one I was looking for: Overham's Super-hot Chilli Powder. It was in a special lead-lined cask, and the label warned that any more than a teaspoonful could have extremely serious consequences for which the manufacturer would not take the blame. I just hoped it would have serious consequences for our slug!

Emptying my explorer's kit onto the floor, I packed the chilli barrel into my rucksack and ran back outside. Captain Cut-throat was still shouting orders and bravely trying to hack at the giant slug with her cutlass, but she couldn't get close enough because of the sticky slime that oozed towards her.

I knew I'd never be able to throw the powder far enough to reach the slug, so I dashed across to the mainmast, thinking I could climb up onto the rigging and then swing out above the sticky creature. But the slug turned towards the mast at exactly the same time and I pulled up short – there was no way I was going to risk climbing straight past its jaws!

I looked around desperately for another route up into the rigging. And that's when I spotted the pirates' plank wobbling over the water. It gave me an idea. A scary one, but it was just about the only chance of saving the ship (and me!) from

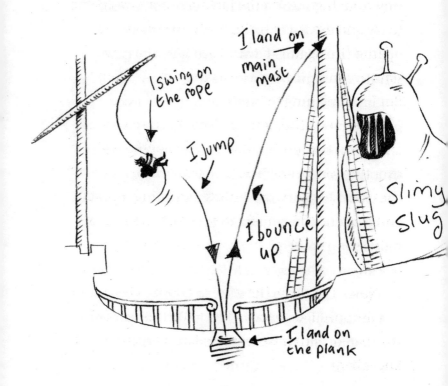

I swing on the rope

I land on main mast

I jump

I bounce up

Slimy Slug

I land on the plank

the deadly slug attack. So, picking up a coil of rope, I dashed to the foremast and started to scramble up the rigging.

Up I went until I reached the cross-spar and then shuffled my way along to the end. Then, tying one end of my rope to the cross-spar, I took my bearings. Way below on the deck, halfway between me and the mainmast, I could see the pirates' plank sticking out over the water. It looked tiny from high up on the foremast, but I was going to try and use it as a springboard to launch me up into the rigging of the mainmast, above the slavering slug. It would take pinpoint accuracy. But I had nothing to lose.

Here goes, I thought, and slid off the cross-spar and down the rope, so that I was dangling high over the deck below. Then, by working my legs backward and forward, I started to swing. Forward and back, further and further, until I was sailing right out over the pirates' plank, twenty metres below.

'Now!' I cried and let go of the rope. 'Geronimo!'

I dropped like a stone. 'Please let this work,' I whispered, with my eyes closed, feet together and knees bent.

I landed right on the end of the plank and – *BOING!* – '*Yahoo!*'

The plank catapulted me high into the air, over the waving horns of the slug and into the rigging of the mainmast. I had made it! Gasping for breath, I shrugged off my rucksack and loosened the lid on the chilli cask.

The slug had seen me, and with a horrible gurgling sound it turned, stretching up towards me in the rigging. My feet were just above its slobbering jaws and the disgusting thing was stretching higher and higher. I had no time to lose. I opened the cask and tipped out the super-hot chilli powder.

For a moment I thought I'd missed, but then a great orange cloud filled the air and the chilli whumped onto the slug's tail like a flour bomb.

There was a moment's silence and then: '*Roarrr!*' The fiery powder started to burn the slug's behind!

I shouldn't think many people have heard a slug roar, but it is a dreadful sound. The creature twisted and turned in a sticky pool of its own slime. It whipped its tail about, trying to cool it down. But there was no way that a little flapping was going to cool down a whole cask of Overham's. So, in desperation, the slug rolled off the side of the ship and writhed frantically around in the cold sea.

As the *Betty Mae* rocked and rolled and finally righted herself, the giant slug swam away, honking in embarrassment.

I had done it! I had saved the ship, and everyone's life! Now, perhaps, I would be given my freedom and my phone as a reward . . .

'Charlie!' shouted Captain Cut-throat from below.

'Yes, Captain?' I answered expectantly.

'Get down here and clean up this mess!'

Some Worrying News

Today I woke up to brilliant sunshine, shimmering on the water like melted gold. The air was clean and clear, and if I hadn't been a captive of a gang of ruthless buccaneers, it would have been a perfect day. The crew sang as they worked and I even found myself humming along with them as I swabbed the decks.

Yo-ho-ho-ing with the rest of the crew, I splashed a bucket of water across the boards to rinse them. Suddenly Captain Cut-throat marched across the deck, splattering my nice clean floor with her dirty footprints. The ever-faithful Bobo was at her heels. Climbing the steps to the quarterdeck, she rapped her cutlass on the rails.

'Listen up, me hearties,' she roared. 'I've got some bad news and some good news.' The other pirates gathered round. 'I've just been down in the hold, and the bad news is that we still haven't got enough treasure.'

'Shame!' cried the pirates.

'The good news is . . . we will have to steal some more!'

'Hooray!'

'Set a course for Spangelimar, the jewel of the Indigo Ocean.'

'Hooray!' roared the pirates again as they raced around carrying out their orders.

My heart leaped. If the pirates were raiding a port, then I might have a chance to escape at last! But how could I persuade the captain to take me along with the raiding party?

As Cut-throat marched past, I puffed out my chest and cleared my throat.

She paused and looked me slowly up and down. 'You'll have to get ready for tomorrow, Charlie,' she said finally.

'You mean you're taking me with you?' I gasped, scarcely able to believe my luck.

'Ha!' she roared as Bobo poked her big blue tongue out at me. 'You don't think I'd take a squirt like you, do you? You have to earn the right to be a pirate and come on a raid. And that means a lot more than scaring off one chubby old sea slug! No, you'll stay here, under guard; but we'll need a hundred and fifty packed lunches to take with us, so you'd better get started as soon as you've finished the deck.' And with that the captain stomped away, a sniggering Bobo at her heels.

A hundred and fifty packed lunches? I groaned loudly. Then I had a thought. If the pirates planned on making a raid tomorrow, we must already be close to land. And tonight they'd be busy getting everything ready . . .

Now was the perfect time to try an escape!
But how . . . ?

A Near Miss

I carried on with my chores, racking my brain for an escape plan. The first problem was how to get out of my locked room. Could I slip out when Mop-head brought me my disgusting dinner? No, that was no good. She would be sure to raise the alarm. Somehow I would have to get a key. Then I remembered the chains that held me fast every night: I would need some gunpowder too! And then I would need to retrieve my phone and find a way to get off the ship . . . There was so much to do and so little time!

I went to empty the slop bucket over the side, and as I tipped out the dirty water, a cry came up from below.

'Careful, you blithering nuisance!'

I peered over the side. There, in a small dinghy tied alongside, was Dog-breath Dinah, one of the least popular members of the crew. She was busy scraping barnacles off the side of the ship – a job so horrible that I'm surprised the captain hadn't got me doing it!

As the *Betty Mae* sped through the choppy

seas towards
Spangelimar,
Dinah had to
brace herself in
the little bucking
dinghy, scraping
at the barnacle-
encrusted hull.

Dog-Breath Dinah

'Sorry, Dog-
breath,' I said
and hid a big smile, because Dog-breath's dinghy
would be perfect for my escape.

Suddenly a loud humming made me turn
back. It sounded as if a huge swarm of bees was
approaching but, as I watched, a most unusual
flying fish rose over the rails. It hovered in mid-air,
a few metres from my face. Large-eyed and brightly
coloured, the comical little fish buzzed around on
propeller-shaped fins, like a miniature helicopter. I
had never seen anything like it before.

'Look,' I cried as the fish stared at me with a
quizzical expression and puffed out its cheeks.

'*Duck!*' somebody shouted.

'No, it's a fish— *Ooof!*' I crashed to the deck as
Mop-head hit me with a fierce rugby tackle.

69

'Hey, what was that for?'

Kate picked herself up and pointed to where a lethal-looking dart was embedded in the mainmast. It was still vibrating.

'You mean the *fish* shot that dart at me?'

'Aye, and they're deadly poisonous.' Kate carefully pulled the dart out of the mast. 'That would have speared you right between the eyes,' she said, fixing me with a dark stare and handing me the dart.

(I've wrapped it up in a T-shirt and stowed it at the bottom of my rucksack – it's the perfect proof that I've sailed strange seas. I can't wait to show everyone back home. Whenever that might be!)

Preparations For Escape

As soon as I'd finished swabbing the deck, I rushed off to the galley and baked twenty loaves for the pirates' sandwiches. Then I got down to more serious business.

First I went to the food store to fill an empty pepperpot. Why? Because to get to the food store I had to go through the armoury, and as I trotted

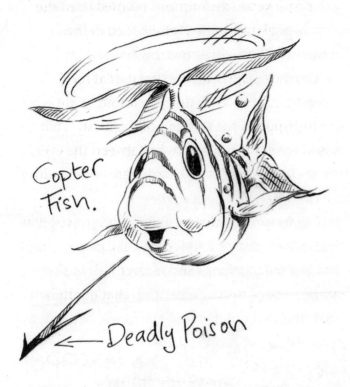

Copter Fish.

← Deadly Poison

innocently past a sack of gunpowder that had been opened ready for tomorrow, I dipped the pepperpot in and filled it to the top. When I returned to the galley and the arms guard asked what I had been doing, I held up the pot.

'Getting pepper for the captain's sandwiches,' I said, and she let me pass.

Then it was straight to the key cupboard that was situated just outside the captain's cabin. I opened the cupboard and looked at the rows of rusting keys that dangled from their hooks. I quickly read the tangle of labels as I scanned the keys row by row:

TREASURE ROOM
CAPTAIN'S CHEST
RUM RATION ROOM
BOBO'S CAGE

There it was! I grabbed the key, but as I did so, a hand grabbed me by the shoulder and I gasped.

'Got you! What are you doing, boy?' growled

the captain. I turned round and held up the key, hiding the label in the palm of my hand.

'Getting the key to the rum room,' I said nervously. 'To give you some extra rum with your packed lunches.'

The captain eyed me and then grinned and patted me on the shoulder. 'Good thinking, Charlie,' she said. 'A little Dutch courage on such occasions is never wasted. Carry on.' And I darted down the corridor and back to the galley.

Once there, I flicked through my recipes until I found one for Captain Cut-throat's favourite jaw-breaker toffee, then put a pan on to boil. Quickly I poured in the necessary ingredients and turned to my next task. I found a large cake of kitchen soap and split it down the middle with my penknife. Then I placed the key between the two halves and pressed them tightly together. When I took the key out, it left a perfect impression in the soap. I tied the two halves back together and then removed the pan of jaw-breaking toffee that was bubbling on the stove. I carefully poured it into a hole I'd made in the soap, so that the toffee ran down into the mould of the key, and then waited for it to set.

A little while later, when I pulled the soap apart, there, in the middle, was a perfect copy of the key to my lockup made of toffee! Just like this:

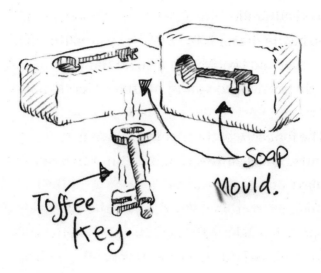

Toffee key.

Soap Mould.

Brilliant!

All I had to do then was put the real key back on its hook before it was missed, hide the toffee key in a spare sandwich and leave that in the scraps cupboard for Kate to find.

Now it's nearly midnight and Kate should be here soon. I'd better finish this entry, pack my rucksack and wait . . .

A Midnight Snack

The minutes ticked slowly by as the noise of the
pirates faded and then stopped. They took to their
bunks early, following orders to get a good night's
sleep before the raid. The *Betty Mae* sliced through
the waves and I could hear an irregular knocking as
the dinghy nudged against her sides. Good – it was
still there.

The footsteps of the night watchwoman
sounded above my head, and the ship groaned and
creaked, but all else was quiet.

Come on, Kate, I said to myself, but nothing
happened for a long time. Then a shuffle, the click
of the lock and the dull glow of a shaded candle as
my door swung open.

'Kate?' I said.

'I've got your scraps, boy,' she replied.

She scampered across the floor and put a plate
down beside me. Thank goodness! As well as
a piece of half-chewed pork pie, there was the
sandwich that I had prepared earlier.
I thanked Kate, but as usual the
strange girl left without a
smile or another word.

Escape From The Lockup

Quickly I felt in my pocket for the pepperpot and folded the bottom of my left trouser leg back, exposing the heavy manacle that chained my ankle to the old oak beam. I wished I could pick locks. It would save a whole heap of trouble. I vowed that this was a skill I would practise and practise if I ever got the chance.

Carefully I sprinkled the gunpowder into the hole of the lock. Then I cut a length of string from the ball in my explorer's kit, rubbed some gunpowder into it, and poked this into the lock to act as a fuse. Finally I reached right down to the bottom of my rucksack.

There I felt a walnut-sized piece of hardened chewing gum. That was where I stuck it if I wanted to save my gum for later. This was much, much later, but I popped it straight into my mouth – and, yes, it was disgusting! It cracked between my teeth and I didn't think it was going to be any use, but as I chewed and chewed, the lump of gum gradually softened and I packed it into the hole to form a seal. I was ready!

Taking my candle, I touched the flame to my homemade fuse. It sparked and spat and I screwed my eyes tight shut as the flame ran down the fuse towards the hole . . .

A muffled bang filled the room, and – 'Aaagh!' – it felt as if someone in a pair of football boots had kicked me on the anklebone. But the manacle fell apart with a clatter and I was free!

BOOF!

I opened my sandwich, retrieved the toffee key and hobbled over to the door. The toffee was rock-hard and I hoped it wouldn't shatter as I turned it in the lock. But luckily the confectionery key turned easily, and with a clunk the door opened and I stepped out into the deserted corridor.

There was one more thing I had to do before I left – get my phone back. It was my only link with home and there was no way I was going to leave it behind. Of course, this meant I would have to steal it from under Cut-throat's nose as she lay sleeping in her hammock, so I quietly limped up to her cabin.

Midnight Robbery

The door creaked as I eased it open and, crouching, slipped inside the captain's cabin. I could hear her snoring. A lamp was turned down but still burning, and when my eyes grew accustomed to the gloom, I could see her lying on her tummy, one arm dangling over the side of the hammock clutching an empty bottle of rum. Good – she should be sleeping soundly.

I crept across the uneven floor, hardly daring to breathe, until I was standing right next to her. The captain had a nightcap pulled down over her eyes and was snorting and grunting like a pig with a blocked nose. And there, poking out from under her pillow, were my phone and charger!

I started to ease them out as gently as possible from under Cut-throat's pillow. If she opened her eyes now, I was a goner! No amount of fibbing would explain what I was doing. But slowly, millimetre by millimetre, I edged the phone towards me.

'*No!*' yelled Captain Cut-throat, and I froze in terror. 'No, me hearties, hang 'em all!' I breathed a sigh of relief; Cut-throat was still asleep and in the middle of a dream. I pulled the phone free, pocketed it and, with my heart in my mouth, crept back outside.

Over & The Side

The night was cloudy and dark; a fine, misty rain soaked the air, making the deck slick and slippery. Keeping to the blackest shadows, I crept along the quarterdeck. Just above me I could see the silhouette of the first mate as an even denser black against the night sky. Peering over the ship's side, I could just make out the dark smudge of the dinghy below, where the waves bubbled silver against the ship's hull. I swung my leg over the rails, found the rope ladder with my foot and started to climb down.

With the rain and the wind and my aching ankle, it was a dangerous climb, and halfway down . . . I slipped. My hands grabbed at the rungs, but everything was too wet and I fell. I waited for the impact as I hit the dinghy. But – '*Ooof!*' – it was a surprisingly soft landing!

'Ow! OK, OK, I surrender,' a voice shouted into the night, and what I thought must be a pile of sails shifted underneath me. It was another pirate! Footsteps sounded from the deck above and a lantern was held out over the side.

'What's going on down there?' came the first mate's voice. 'Stay where you are. You're under arrest!'

The Captain Cogitates

'What's the meaning of this?' roared Captain Cut-throat when we were hauled up in front of her, Dog-breath scowling and me limping on my bad ankle. She sat at the table in her cabin in her nightgown and cap, still half asleep. Things couldn't get much worse, I thought, as the captain glared at us. I had been on the verge of escaping from this floating dustbin and now it looked as if I could end up swinging from a yardarm after all.

'Dog-breath Dinah caught trying to escape, Cap'n,' said the first mate. 'Seems that the cabin boy here overpowered her and stopped her getting away with this.' A heavy sack was dumped on the table with an ominous telltale clink.

What was this? The first mate thought I had prevented Dinah from escaping? I held my breath and waited to see what happened.

'Is this true?' demanded the captain, tipping the sack up and spilling a cascade of gold coins onto the table.

'Aye, and I would have got clean away if it hadn't been for this infernal nuisance,' growled Dinah. 'I've had enough of your bullying ways – always being called names and given the dirtiest jobs. So I decided to take what I was due and make a getaway. I was just about to pull on the oars when this twit dropped out of the sky and flattened me.'

The captain ran her fingers through the gold. 'You've broken every rule of the pirates' code,' she said. 'And for that there is no excuse.'

'Big deal,' scoffed Dog-breath Dinah.

At that the captain reached across to a lever on her desk and pulled.

'Aaaargh!' screamed Dinah as a trapdoor opened beneath her feet and she dropped into the black sea below. I gasped and looked down at my own feet and, sure enough, I could see the outline of another trapdoor.

Dinah fell through the trapdoor into the sea below...

'And now we come to you . . .' said Captain Cut-throat, stroking a lever on the other side of her desk and staring at me with her ice-cold eyes. 'How come you managed to get out of your locked room and tackle a big, brawny pirate single handed . . .? And why would a little goody-two-shoes like you decide to help us anyway?'

'Well . . .' I gulped, knowing that what I said now would decide whether I lived or was plunged into the cruel sea. How good a liar could I be? 'I, um, I was woken by some strange noises in the next room, Dinah's room. I know she sleeps there because the rest of the crew won't let her sleep with them, on account of her being so smelly. I could hear her moving about . . . um, dragging something heavy. I knew that all the crew had been ordered to bed early, so I decided to investigate. I saw she was trying to escape. I had to act quickly. I was worried that she might be going to warn the people of Spangelimar. And I thought if I could stop her, you might trust me to come on the raid.'

The captain narrowed her eyes. 'How did you manage to get out?' she demanded.

'I, um . . . I can pick locks,' I lied. 'I used to be a safebreaker before you found me. And another thing,' I added, knowing that if the mobile was found on me, I'd swing for sure: 'I found this in Dinah's boat,' and I placed the mobile and charger on the desk. I couldn't believe that after all the danger I'd gone through to get my mobile back, I had to hand it over to Cut-throat again!

The captain stared, her eyebrows rising and knotting as she thought. Her hand was still on the lever and my legs wobbled like jelly as I waited for the floor to give way. Then, all of a sudden, she let her hand fall and slapped the table.

'Good job, Charlie,' she said. 'A very good job indeed. I may have misjudged you, boy, and your skills as a pick-a-lock may come in very useful. Consider yourself promoted to ordinary pirate. Go back to your cabin and get some sleep, for you've earned the right to come on tomorrow's raid!'

And that's where I am now. Not chained any more, but lying in a brand new hammock! It's brilliantly comfortable, but I'm still a bit wobbly from my night's adventures. I can't believe that

I didn't get found out, and that I might even get another chance to escape tomorrow. Maybe I'll even be able to turn the pirates in for a fat reward!

I wish I could sleep, but butterflies begin flapping around my tummy every time I close my eyes. Who knows what will happen?

(Note: After my fib about being an expert lock-picker, the captain has had my door secured by a heavy wooden bar!)

A Pirate Raid

Oh boy! Today did *not* go as planned at all. I'm still shaking from fear and excitement, and my racing heart is only just starting to slow down. I might be living with some of the most feared pirates on the ocean, each day filled with danger and treachery, but at least I'm never bored!

We woke very early and, under cover of the morning mist, manoeuvred the *Betty Mae* off the headland at Spangelimar. There, final preparations were made and the pirates honed their cutlasses to an air-zinging sharpness.

What a brilliant bit of proof of my time on a pirate ship. I found this scrap of paper on the floor. It looks like a pirate started the crossword - and then gave up!

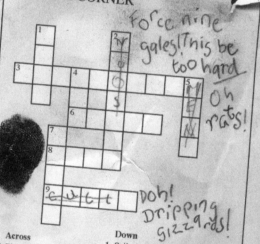

Pirate Weekly

PUZZLE CORNER

Force nine gales! This be too hard

Oh rats!

Doh! Dripping gizzards!

Across
3. Pirate's flag (5-5)
6. Walk the ----- (5)
8. Another word for the ship's wheel (4)
9. A type of sword (5)

Down
1. Sailor's call: 'Ship --- (4)
2. You hang people from this (7)
4. What waves do on the shore (3)
5. On board vermin (4)
7. Where pirates keep their treasure (5)

TERRO...

It was...
had be...
the Po...
believe...
Cutthr...
gang of...
Thief ta...
would n...
had cap...
If you h...
about the...
Joseph G...
Tortilla...

SUNNY

We shoul...
in for sor...
weather...
HOT! H...

In readiness for their trip, the ladies donned their most fashionable frocks. And what a sight they were! I had never seen them in dresses before, and I can't say they looked any better than when wearing their pirate gear. They didn't smell any better either, despite having doused themselves in strong-smelling perfume. They often did this to save themselves having to wash.

Rawcliffe Annie, ready for the raid!

It never worked, and if you stood downwind from them, they had the rich, musty smell of a herd of gnu.

They wore their skirts for a reason, though: the folds of fabric covered their swords and daggers and pistols. And under their bonnets they'd hidden powder horns and lead shot. Even I was given a cutlass, secreting it under a long heavy coat that the pirates lent me, and as I fastened the belt around my waist, I saw Cut-throat slip my mobile into her handbag and snap it shut. If I *was* going to make an escape, I would need to pinch it from her bag first!

Then, lowering the Jolly Roger and hoisting the innocent flag of the Women's Institute, we sailed into the harbour.

The Plan

Captain Cut-throat ordered us all into large rowing boats and I sat nervously between her and Rawcliffe Annie as we crossed the water, wondering if I'd have the chance to grab my phone and make a dash for freedom, or if I'd be forced to make my debut as a pillaging thief.

On the way Captain Cut-throat explained her sneaky plan. The pirates were to pretend to be on a shopping trip but would really be carefully positioning themselves all around the market square.

'Then I will let out a blood-curdling yell,' she said. 'And while everyone is distracted, you girls draw your weapons and we've got 'em! Then all we have to do is empty their purses. Easy-peasy!'

'What about me?' I asked her nervously.

'Well, as we are all supposed to be ordinary ladies out on a shopping trip, you'd better pretend to be my son,' she replied. 'And then, at the end, you can take round the sack for all the kind people to fill.'

'I can't rob a crowd of innocent people!' I protested. Then, seeing the captain's scowl, I

89

added, 'I mean . . . not as it's my first time. What if I got it wrong? Er . . . how about I stay and guard the rowing boats instead?'

Captain Cut-throat's hand closed round the collar of my coat and I was lifted as easily as a baby from the floor of the rowing boat. With her nose just a millimetre away from mine, she stared straight into my eyes.

'Unless you want your gizzard a-dangling from the tip of my sword, I don't think you have any choice, dear boy.'

I swallowed hard. It looked as if I was going to be a pirate whether I liked it or not!

Sword

gizzard!

Daylight Robbery!

My heart raced and my palms sweated as our little rowing boat scraped the wall of the quay and we moored. Captain Cut-throat took my hand and gave it a squeeze, whether of encouragement or as a warning I didn't know, and we walked along the stone jetty and across the cobbled harbour. My ankle was feeling much better, and I looked around nervously, trying to see a way to escape. But the captain had me in an iron grip and there was no way I could make a dash for freedom.

I thought about crying out, 'Kidnap!' but as soon as the thought crossed my mind, the captain squeezed my hand even harder, and when I glanced up at her, she was holding her shawl slightly open: tucked under her armpit I could see her jewel-encrusted dagger, glinting. It was as if she could read my mind: I quickly gave up the idea of yelling out. I was off the ship, but still very much a prisoner, and besides, the captain still had my precious mobile and I needed it back.

We seated ourselves on the picturesque

quayside and ate our packed lunches while Cut-throat scanned the scene for any possible trouble. But nobody took the slightest notice of us and, satisfied, the captain whispered to us to follow.

We promenaded genteelly through twisting alleyways, up flights of steps and out into the market square.

The pirates' plan was working. The dandies of the town tipped their hats and said, 'Good morning, ladies.' But when the pirates turned and smiled and the young men saw their weather-beaten, toothless faces, they made a quick apology and hurried away. I desperately wanted to cry out, but the captain still had my mobile – and her long, sharp dagger.

As the pirates wandered through the market square, casually browsing among the stalls, I took a good look around. I was in a very tricky situation and needed a way out. On one side the square ended in a low wall that looked out over the bay below. Amongst the boats that dotted the bay I could see the *Betty Mae* at anchor, looking small and dishevelled next to her neighbour – a gleaming golden galleon. At each end of the wall stood a light cannon, and I knew immediately what I must do. I would have to blast the *Betty Mae* out of action and prevent the pirates getting away.

Just then, Captain Cut-throat let out a blood-curdling yell. 'Help! Stop, thieves! Please help a poor defenceless lady!' she screamed, and the shoppers rushed over to help. I took my chance to slip away through the crowd and darted over to the cannon, half hidden behind a market stall.

Blasted Out Of The Water

'Where are they?' cried the townsfolk. 'Where are the thieves?'

'Why, they're all around you.' The captain smiled, sweeping her arm theatrically through the air.

The townsfolk turned to find themselves surrounded by a forest of swords, pistols and cutlasses.

As the pirates herded their victims together, I quickly rammed a bag of gunpowder from the powder chest down the barrel of the gun. A cannonball and a piece of wadding followed. I had watched the pirates during their firing practice, so I knew which order these things went in, but I had no idea how much powder to use. I just hoped it was enough to fire the ball.

'Now, if you wouldn't mind emptying your pockets, ladies and gentlemen, my young friend, Black-hearted Charlie, will pass among you,' Captain Cut-throat was declaring, holding out a calico bag. 'This bag will need filling before we can take our leave. Charlie, if you please . . . Charlie? *Charlie?* Where are you?'

With shaking hands I poured some powder into the firing hole and scrabbled in the chest for the tinderbox. Then I noticed a large, terrifying-looking man in a long black coat step out of the crowd and stand in front of Captain Cut-throat. A nervous hush settled over the square, and a spasm of fear shuddered down my spine.

'Remember me, Cut-throat?' the man snarled. 'I hear you took a friend of mine for a walk recently.'

'Craik!' spat the captain. 'Turncoat Craik! Well, it will be a pleasure to relieve you of your possessions, you dog.'

'Take what you like, but you won't get very far. My ship is anchored below and has enough guns to blast you to kingdom come.' The man smiled. 'You won't make it beyond the harbour walls.'

The captain looked worried at this news, and I thought it was time to make doubly sure that the *Betty Mae* couldn't escape, so I sparked the flint against the steel and the fuse started to spit and smoke.

'There's no need to worry,' I shouted, aiming the cannon directly at the *Betty Mae*. 'They won't be going anywhere!'

Everyone stared at me.

'What's going on, Charlie?' demanded Captain Cut-throat.

'Well—' I began, but as I walked behind the cannon, the cutlass in my belt slipped, got caught between my legs and tripped me up. '*Oof!*' I fell against the heavy gun, the barrel swung round and *BOOM!* the cannon fired with a mighty explosion that echoed around the square and shook the market stalls. I had used more than enough powder!

'Stay where you are,' the captain shouted at Craik and pushed her way through the crowd, reaching me just as the cannonball shattered the side . . . of the fancy golden galleon! Immediately, amid billows of yellow smoke, her crew poured onto the deck and jumped overboard into the water. Somehow my cannonball had sparked a fire in their ammunition store, and as the sailors swam to safety on the far side of the bay, the ship was ripped apart in a series of deafening explosions. Oh, no! What had I done?

'My ship!' screamed Craik, shaking with anger.

'Oh Charlie,' said Captain Cut-throat, putting her arm around my shoulders as a huge cloud of smoke and sparks shot into the sky. 'What magnificent shooting! Now, let's finish what we came to do.'

BOOM!

Craik Makes A Promise

Trembling with nerves, and not daring to look at anyone, I pushed through the crowd, holding the mouth of the calico bag open wide. It filled quickly to the chink of doubloons and guineas, bracelets and rings.

As I passed Craik in his black velvet coat, he grabbed me by the shoulder and I glanced up at his large, unforgiving face. Holding up a fat purse, he looked me straight in the eye. My tummy churned with fear and my legs turned to jelly.

'I hope you can run, Black-hearted Charlie,' he said , dropping his purse into my open sack.

'I will see you hang,'
said Craik

'For I will follow you to the ends of the earth, and when I catch you, I will see you hang.' His eyes sparked with fury and I knew he meant every word.

'Charlie, what's keeping you?' yelled Captain Cut-throat. 'Let's go!'

Still shaking and speechless, I slung the heavy sack over my shoulder and pushed back out through the silent crowd. All the pirates had gathered together, weapons trained on the angry mob. Some of my shipmates were carrying sides of pork or lamb that they had taken from the market stalls. Others had stolen casks of rum and wine or fancy goods. Carefully we backed out of the square into one of the narrow alleyways that led down to the harbour.

'So long, folks,' cried the captain, and as soon as we had turned a corner, we ran! With a roar, the crowd was after us.

A Narrow Escape

We poured through the lanes and down flights of steps with the townsfolk hard on our heels. There were so many of us rushing to get away that we became jammed in the narrow entrance to one lane. We pushed and shoved as the crowd got nearer and nearer, but we were stuck fast. At the head of the crowd was Craik, and he was looking straight at me. I shoved with all my might, and as the man's large, bony hand closed once again on my shoulder, the plug of pirates forced its way free and we shot down the alley like corks from a bottle.

'I'll see you hang, boy!' the black-coated man yelled after me and, in a moment of relief and bravado, I turned and shouted back, 'You've got to catch me first!' and all the pirates cheered.

We rushed onto the quayside, the angry mob still hot on our heels. Now we were out in the open, our pursuers were able to load, aim and fire without hitting each other. Red-hot bullets were soon whizzing past our ears.

'Jump!' shouted Captain Cut-throat, and we leaped into the rowing boats, where the pirates' best rowers were ready for a quick getaway. Amid shouts, shots and cries, they pulled for the safety of our galleon with all their might. I collapsed with relief when we'd clambered safely back aboard the *Betty Mae*.

'Well done, Charlie!' roared Captain Cut-throat. 'It took some nerve, blasting Craik's ship like that.'

'The man in the long black coat?'

'Aye, lad. That was the notorious Joseph Craik, thief-taker extraordinaire!'

I sat down heavily as a prickling heat flushed through my body. A thief-taker was an expert in tracking down escaped convicts, and this one had just vowed to catch me. I was a wanted man.

'Cheer up,' said the captain. 'Why, you're one of us now!'

As the town's defensive guns erupted with a roar, and cannonballs smashed into the water around us, the Jolly Roger was hoisted once again and we sailed out to sea and away.

And now, for the first time since boarding the *Betty Mae*, I'm writing up my journal, sitting in my smelly quarters with my DOOR UNLOCKED! I must have earned the pirates' respect . . .

Is this a good or a bad thing? I wonder.

I don't want to end up hanging from a yardarm!

A Celebration

As soon as we had reached safer waters, the pirates celebrated their haul with an enormous feast. They sang songs of the sea, of treachery and death, and I joined in as they raised their hoarse voices to the wind in the night sky.

'We were poor little wives of black-hearted pirates,
Who left us at home, playing at mum,
But now we've become the scourge of the oceans,
So watch your backs and pass me the rum.

'Rum, rum (fresh, slimy gizzards)
Rum, rum (saltwater scum)
Rum, rum (don't spit in the wind, girls)
Rum, rum, just pass me the rum.

'Our wake-up call is the roar of the cannon,
The bright, gleaming dagger is our best chum,
That's how we've become the scourge of the oceans,
It's all over for you, now pass me the rum.

'Rum, rum (new golden guineas)
Rum, rum (head in the noose)
Rum, rum (over the side, girls)
Rum, rum, now pass me the juice.'

At the end of the meal Captain Cut-throat called me over and gave me a goblet full of the black, spicy drink.

'Raise your glasses to Charlie Small!' she roared. 'A true pirate and the latest member of our gang.'

The pirates drained their glasses, and amid cheers and belches I held my nose, raised my glass and took a glug . . . Aargh! The drink exploded in my tummy like liquid dynamite and I doubled up, clutching my guts.

'Good old Charlie!' the pirates laughed. 'We'll make a pirate of you yet.' And then I promptly passed out!

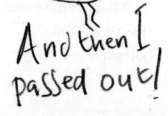

And then I passed out!

Searching The Ship

Being a boy, I know I'll never be completely trusted by the pirates, but I have earned their respect and now have the freedom to explore the ship from top to bottom.

I'm still desperate to escape. So I've been searching the *Betty Mae*'s dark, twisting corridors, looking for anything that I could use. So far I haven't found a single thing.

Tomorrow I plan to search deep in the murky hold where the pirates almost never go.

Some Special Finds

Today has been a day of marvellous discoveries! Down in the bowels of the ship I found a junk room packed to the rafters with stuff the pirates didn't want. Alongside all the boxes of soap there were odd bits of machinery, broken clocks and swords and bits of skeleton, most of it rotting in the stinking bilge-water that slopped around the bottom of the ship.

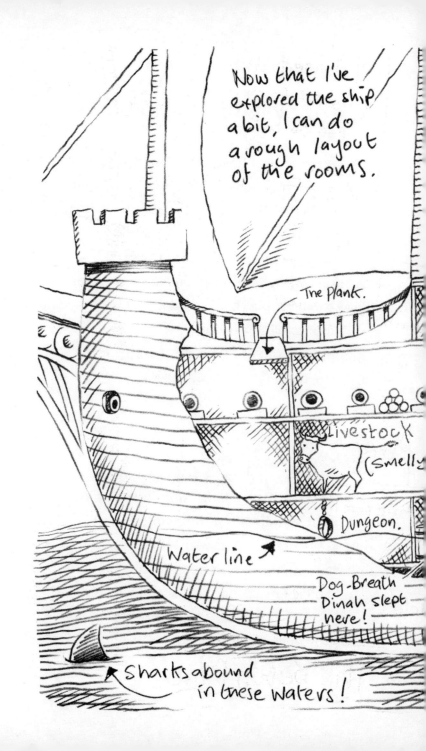

I rummaged through the piles of junk, trying to find something that I could use to help me escape. I had been thinking I could maybe build a raft like the one I began my adventures on, so I started collecting planks and sheets of rotted sail. Then, in a far corner, I saw something that had my heart leaping.

As the beam of my torch played across a pile of boxes, it picked out a label that read: *Property of Jakeman's Works*. The box had never been opened. Fantastic! I thought. Jakeman had built my dear old friend the steam-powered rhinoceros, which had saved my life on the great golden plain before I'd been made king of the gorillas. Excitedly I jammed the hoofpick on my penknife under the lid and heaved down; with a loud crack the lid leaped free of the box.

I hurriedly pushed aside some straw packing . . . and saw not one, but two astonishing inventions. A label on the underside of the lid read:

Jakeman's Powder-Propelled Jet Swordfish
(with clockwork limpet drills)

The swordfish looked like a grinning torpedo.

Its articulated body of polished steel panels gleamed in the gloom of the storeroom. It tapered to a wide, flat tail at one end and a long, vicious-looking corkscrew nose at the other, and was every bit as impressive as the rhino.

I studied the instruction manual, full of intricate diagrams, and, oh boy, it was great stuff! There were two handles behind its head and two stirrups near the tail, and by using Jakeman's patented jet-powder for fuel, the swordfish could speed someone through the water at fifty knots.

The right handle was the throttle, like on a motorbike, and when you twisted it, a valve was opened, letting water drip into a tank and onto Jakeman's special powder. This caused a chemical reaction, making lots of gas, which was forced down an exhaust pipe at great pressure into the sea, thrusting the swordfish forward. It could dive, it could turn and it could leap; I could already see myself whizzing through the waves to freedom!

I have torn out the diagram of the swordfish to show what it looked like:

The clockwork limpets lay nestled next to the swordfish. I'd heard of limpets and knew they were small sea creatures with a conical shell that

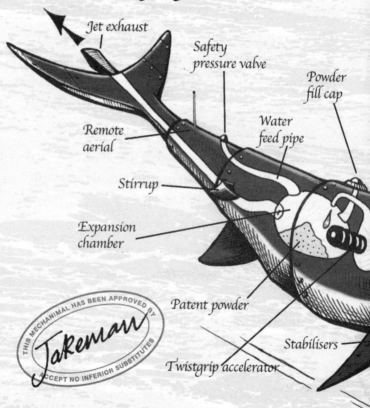

JAKEMAN'S POWDER-PROPELLED JET SWORDFISH

A Sea-going Mechanimal

Jet exhaust

Safety pressure valve

Powder fill cap

Remote aerial

Water feed pipe

Stirrup

Expansion chamber

Patent powder

Stabilisers

Twistgrip accelerator

THIS MECHANIMAL HAS BEEN APPROVED BY
Jakeman
ACCEPT NO INFERIOR SUBSTITUTES

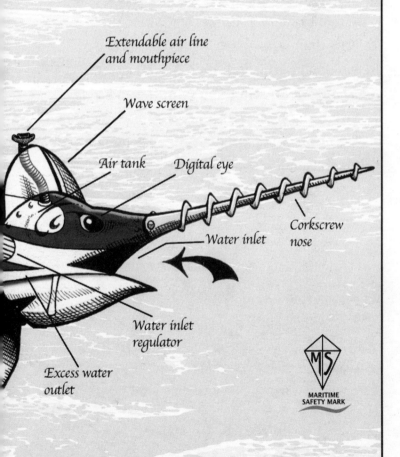

STATS:
Max speed: 50 knots
320 brake fishpower
0–50 in 3 seconds

Chemical formula for Jakeman's gas
producing powder:
$NaHCO3+R2UST3+H20 = FzzzzPop!$

Patent No. 113236

Extendable air line
and mouthpiece

Wave screen

Air tank   Digital eye

Corkscrew
nose

Water inlet

Water inlet
regulator

Excess water
outlet

MARITIME
SAFETY MARK

clung to rocks. These did
the same: they were
small metal domes
with a rubber
seal running

Limpet at the
seaside (actual size).

Rock

around their base that you could stick to almost
anything by pushing down a lever that created
a vacuum inside. The domes contained three
rotating diamond-coated blades on the end of
an extendable arm, and when wound up, the
clockwork motor sent them spinning and slicing
into whatever surface the domes were stuck
to. They were some sort of drilling device, and
although I couldn't see how they could possibly
help me, I decided to take them as well.

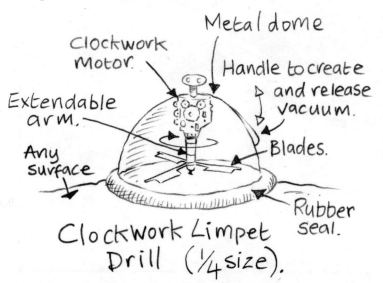

Metal dome

Clockwork
Motor.

Handle to create
and release
vacuum.

Extendable
arm.

Any
surface

Blades.

Rubber
seal.

Clockwork Limpet
Drill (¼ size).

I hope the jet-powered swordfish still works, for tonight, if I can retrieve my mobile and charger from Cut-throat, I plan to ride the swordfish across the sea to freedom, and this time tomorrow the *Betty Mae*, the pirates and the thief-taker will be far, far behind me!

Escape At Last

Right, everything's ready. I'm just packing my rucksack ... Oh, darn it, something is happening up top. I'll have to go and investigate ...

It's all about to kick off. More later...

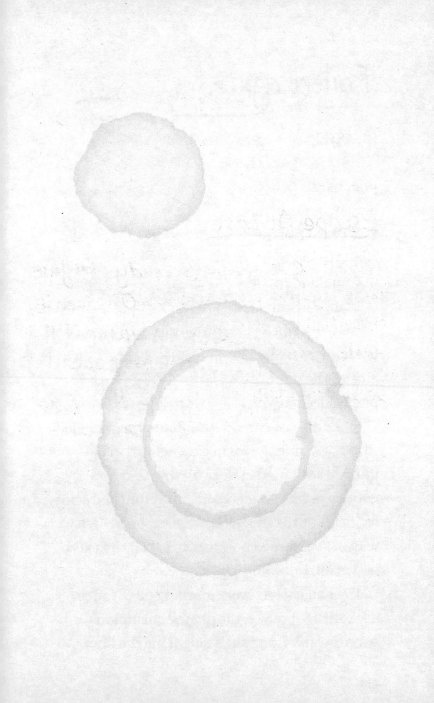

Foiled again!

DISASTER!

Am I free? Am I heck! I can hardly believe it myself, but I am now FIRST MATE of the *Betty Mae*, second in command to Captain Cut-throat herself! It seems the harder I try to escape, the more of a pirate I become!

It was hot enough to boil your eyeballs!

Since my last entry in this journal we've sailed through raging storms in treacherous, shark-infested seas; fried under a blazing sun, hot enough to boil your eyeballs; and crunched across ice-fields until our rigging was festooned with icicles. I've learned how to spit, eat raw fish and, best of all, to sword-fight.

I've had lessons every morning on the main deck with Sabre Sue, the pirates' champion swordswoman, and she's taught me the finer

points of 'The Chop' or 'The Windmill' while the
rest of the crew gather round to cheer and laugh
at my efforts. I've practised feinting and parrying,
thrusting and sidestepping until I reckon I'm
nearly as good as Sabre Sue herself. I can even
skewer a ship's biscuit from a hundred paces with
my cutlass!

Sabre Sue
demonstrates
"The Windmill"

How did all this happen? I keep asking myself. How did I end up the second most important pirate on the most feared pirate ship sailing the Pangaean Ocean? It's absurd! But it all started the very night I had planned to escape . . .

I had hidden the jet-powered swordfish under some sacking on deck and was waiting anxiously for nightfall. My rucksack was packed and ready and I was waiting for a chance to slip in and retrieve my mobile from Cut-throat's cabin. But as the sun dipped towards the horizon of a wave-scalloped sea, a call came from up in the crow's-nest.

'*Ship ahoy!*'

I rushed to the ship's rails with the rest of the crew and, sure enough, there it was, emerging from the gloom off our port bow – a large naval ship of the line, bristling with scores of heavy cannon. And she was heading straight towards us!

Under Attack!

Captain Cut-throat leaped to the poop deck and started barking out orders. Sails were trimmed, ropes tightened and the arms store broken open. Swords, cutlasses, pistols and blunderbusses were passed quickly down the line until every pirate was armed to the teeth. Me included!

Pirates went clattering down to the gun decks to get the cannon ready for battle. A snarling Bobo was let out of her cage; she climbed onto the rails to scream across the water at the fast-approaching enemy. The closer the ship got, the more impressive she looked. She was fast, heavily armed and crewed by the navy's finest.

I peered through my telescope and my heart stopped. For there, craning forward over the bows, was Joseph Craik, and he was looking straight at me. He was too far away for me to hear him, but I could read his lips.

'I spy you, Black-hearted Charlie, and I'll see you twitch on the end of a rope!'

What was I going to do? If I tried to escape now, both the pirates and Craik would be after me. I racked my brains for a plan. Then, as the enemy's cannon roared into life and cannonballs peppered the sea around us, I remembered Jakeman's clockwork limpets. Could they help? I rushed over to the hidden swordfish and threw back the tarpaulin.

Into The Sea

Panting heavily, I dragged the steel fish over to Captain Cut-throat.

'What's all this?' she cried suspiciously, but I had no time to explain. I told her to lower the fish down to me and then jumped over the side. I hit the water with a splash, gasping with the cold. Seconds later the powder-propelled jet swordfish was lowered into the waves beside me.

As the steel fish floated on the water, its body flexing with the swell, I grabbed hold of the handles on either side of its head before the strength of the waves swept me away. Then, taking a cask full of Jakeman's special jet-powder from my pocket, I slid back a cover on the fish's head and poured it into a hole.

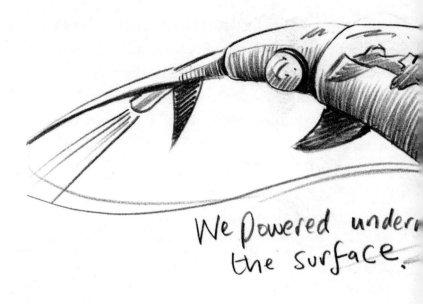

We powered under
the surface.

I gave the throttle a tentative turn, there was a
fizzing noise from inside the metal fish, and as the
gas bubbled out of the exhaust pipe, we shot across
the surface of the sea in the shadow of the *Betty
Mae*. The further I turned the handle, the faster we
went: we sped through the water and the deadly
corkscrew nose of the swordfish started to spin.
Brilliant!

'I'll be watching you, boy,' cried Cut-throat from
the deck of the *Betty Mae*. 'So don't even think
about escaping on that contraption.'

As soon as I rounded the *Betty Mae*'s bows and
was in view of the enemy ship, I pushed down
the nose of the swordfish, took a gulp of air and
we powered below the surface like a torpedo. As I
headed straight towards the bows of the enemy,
I could hear the boom of cannon from above the
surface; I wobbled in the wake of cannonballs
dropping through the sea around me. I opened
the throttle, closed my eyes and hoped that I was
going to reach the naval ship before it blew the
Betty Mae clean out of the water.

Jakeman's Clockwork Limpets

The next thing I knew, the spinning corkscrew nose of the silver swordfish was grinding into the hull of the enemy ship, twisting itself into the wooden sides just below the waterline. It screwed in deep enough to hold us fast, but not enough to do the galleon any serious damage. I shut off the throttle and sat up. My head popped above the choppy surface and I was able to breathe again. Cannons and confusion roared above me as I unclipped the clockwork limpets from the fish and wound them up as far as they would go.

The water surged around me as the galleon sped through the sea, all guns blazing. Smoke billowed from its gun ports and the crack of musket shots filled the air. I had to hurry. Taking a huge gulp of air, I dived under the surface once again. I whacked a limpet drill against the ship and yanked the lever that would clamp it to the wooden hull. I did the same with the other drill. Then, flicking them on, I reversed the swordfish, freeing its nose from the hull, and sped back towards the *Betty Mae*. Both ships were firing round after round from their cannons and the *Betty Mae* was getting badly damaged. But if my plan worked and the limpets chewed through the naval vessel's hull, its crew would be too busy launching lifeboats to think about firing any more cannonballs at our boat.

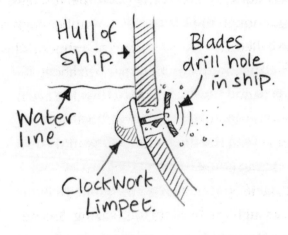

Hull of ship. →

Blades drill hole in ship.

Water line.

Clockwork Limpet.

Up From The Deep!

I powered back through the waves, no longer worried about being seen.

'Get that boy!' I heard Joseph Craik shout, and the next minute bullets were zipping past my ears. I dived, letting the swordfish take me deep into the ocean, under the keel of the *Betty Mae* and up the other side to shelter in the shadow of her huge hulk. I gulped a deep lungful of air and looked up to the deck, where Captain Cut-throat was lowering a rope with a grappling hook to hoist me out. Then I heard a terrible gurgling noise, the sound of rushing water and splitting wood, and a huge cheer went up from the *Betty Mae*.

'It's all over,' cried Cut-throat. 'Their ship is scuppered and they're taking to their lifeboats!' But I knew that it wasn't all over, because now I'd sunk *two* of the thief-taker's ships and I didn't think he was going to forget that in a hurry.

The grappling hook was swinging just above my head and I reached up to grab it. But as I did so, I felt something grip my ankle and I was yanked under the surface with tremendous force!

Down, down I was pulled, through a sea boiling with bubbles, still sitting on the back of the silver swordfish. I tore at the thing gripping my ankle and felt a thick, suckered tentacle. I was in serious trouble. Another tentacle snaked up from the depths, wrapping itself around the

swordfish, and we were pulled deeper into the ocean. As the bubbles cleared, I found myself staring into the eyes of a giant octopus. Some of its many arms, ten metres long, waved with the swell of the sea, while those wrapped around the swordfish and me moved us closer and closer to its vicious, sharp beak of a mouth.

Captain Cutthroat to the rescue

Struggling to hold my breath, I put the swordfish on full throttle but it was no use – the octopus was just too strong. It pulled us right up to its beak, snapping off the front of the steel swordfish and shredding it as easily as industrial steel snips through cloth. I was next, and I shut my eyes as I was swept inside its mouth.

Suddenly the octopus shuddered and loosened its grip! Through the bubbles I saw Captain Cut-throat standing on the grappling hook that had been lowered from the deck of the *Betty Mae*. She had one hand on the rope that reached down from the ship; the other was stretched out towards me.

Looking back at the octopus, I saw a large whaling harpoon sticking out from between its eyes. Black ink poured from the stricken monster as I kicked off from the remains of the swordfish and swam over to the captain, my lungs burning for want of oxygen. As soon as I had Cut-throat's hand, she pulled on the rope and we were hoisted up through the sea.

I couldn't believe it! Captain Cut-throat had saved my life!

We broke through the surface and I gasped and spluttered and coughed, filling my lungs with the cool sea air. Then, as my ears stopped thumping with my racing pulse, I became aware that the whole of the pirate crew, except for Bobo, were peering over the deck of the *Betty Mae*, cheering wildly. I was a hero! And that's how I became first mate on a pirate ship!

Revenge

Well, I never wanted to be first mate, and I still dream of escape, but I must admit that life has been easier since my promotion. My duties as cabin boy have been handed to Bobo, who now has to leave her luxurious cage every morning and scrub the decks, clean the pans and perform all my other duties. Bobo is not a happy monkey and her hatred of me has grown – if that was possible. If she ever gets the chance to mess things up for me, I'm sure she will.

The poor old *Betty Mae* is in a terrible state. Her hull is full of cannonball holes and the top part of her mainmast has been shot clean off. The crow's-nest lies against the rails of the top deck, waiting for a time when the pirates can carry out repairs. But those repairs will have to wait, because Captain Cut-throat is bent on revenge.

'How dare Craik attack us like that!' she fumed. 'Who does he think he is? He needs to be taught a lesson that he'll never forget.'

I thought that having to row all the way back to

Yeah. Let's teach him a lesson!

land with a hundred angry sailors was enough of a lesson for anyone, and I really didn't think the captain should go looking for Craik again, but I didn't dare say that to the pirates.

'Aye, Cap'n. Let's teach him a lesson,' the crew agreed. 'What shall we do?'

The captain didn't need to think. 'Sail to Tortilla,' she said. 'It's the richest city in the region and it's where Craik lives. If we can plunder the town right under his nose, he'll be a laughing stock.'

So, as we've sailed through sun and snow and storms, we've been preparing for our latest, daring raid. I practised my cutlass skills and have been taught to yell with a ferocity that would have an enemy shaking in their boots. I've also kept my promise and spent many hours practising picking locks. If I ever find myself locked up again, I want to be able to escape without having to nearly blow my foot off!

Soon I found I could open the complicated locks on the pirates' treasure chests in a matter of seconds and discovered that the perfect tool was the poisonous dart from the peculiar flying fish that had attacked me. Its strong, flexible shaft

and double barbed tip was perfectly designed
for the job: I decided I must never go anywhere
without it.

The pirates played starfish Frisbee!

Here We go Again

I have no idea if I will get a chance to escape when
we land at Tortilla, so I've decided I need a plan
B. Whenever possible I've been creeping down
into the belly of the ship to build a new getaway
vehicle. I've had to be careful because Bobo has
been watching me more closely than ever. But
luckily she's been too tired after doing all my old
chores to stay awake late into the night. And the
creaks and groans of the ancient ship have covered

up the noise of my hammering, sawing and glueing.

Using an old barrel as a shell, I've cut an opening in one side and fitted a plank of wood for a seat. Then, using some cogs and an old chain, I've built some pedals to drive two paddle wheels made from strips of wood. With nets filled with coconuts to act as floats, I've built a pedalo that I think even Jakeman might be quite proud of! Here's how it works:

I don't think it will stay afloat long on choppy water, so I'm only going to use it if I don't manage to escape in Tortilla. But I feel happier knowing I have another way out if I need it. (So long as Thief-taker Craik doesn't capture me first!)

A Terrible Fix

Oh no! A terrible thing has happened. Captain Cut-throat has been captured – and it's all my fault! Worse still, she had my mobile phone with her when Craik threw her in the lockup! All my plans to escape are on hold again – I have to get my phone back; and besides, Cut-throat saved my life, so I can't just leave her to rot, can I? I *knew* we should never have gone to Tortilla!

As soon as we arrived in port, Cut-throat sent Annie ashore on a recce. After his defeat, she knew that Craik would be desperate to catch our pirate gang, and she was right. Annie returned from town with a poster she had torn from the harbour wall. Captain Cut-throat unfolded it and handed it to me.

This is what it said:

WANTED

For acts of piracy on the High Seas
And in Her Majesty's Colonies

BLACK-HEARTED CHARLIE

PUBLIC ENEMY No.1

A reward of 2,000 Guineas is offered
To anyone supplying information leading to
The capture of this villainous vermin

DEAD OR ALIVE

Joseph Craik

By order of Joseph Craik, thief taker

I was shocked! Me, Charlie Small, the world's most wanted pirate! What would my mum think? Then, with relief, I realized this meant I couldn't possibly go on the raid! For one glorious moment I thought I would be spared the danger of capture or death, and would be able to escape on my pedalo while the others went ashore. But Captain Cut-throat had other ideas.

'I want you at my side, Charlie,' she said as she squeezed into her posh frock. 'You'll just have to go in disguise like us.'

And then she called for the spare dresses!

'No!' I cried. 'You must be joking.' But the captain insisted and I had to try on every one for the pirates and parade up and down the deck as if I was on a catwalk. Finally they agreed on a full-length, green satin dress trimmed with Spanish lace and a matching bonnet. Talk about embarrassing!

And the long skirt was going to make running away almost impossible!

Taken!

I had no chance to make a dash for it anyway. I was wedged between Rawcliffe and Lizzie Hall in the rowing boat, and then the captain insisted I stay close to her as we headed for the market. 'It's your duty as my first mate, Charlie,' she said. And I knew that if I protested, she'd instantly suspect me.

As the pirates pulled their old trick and rounded up the townsfolk, I kept waiting for the thief-taker to appear with an army of soldiers, but we escaped. At least, we did until it came to the getaway.

With bags full of sparkling loot we swarmed through the narrow alleyways back to the harbour, easily outrunning the angry townsfolk. But then we came to a cobbled street and I suddenly discovered how difficult it is to run over cobbles in a long dress and high heels! As we took a corner at high speed, my ankle twisted on the cobbles and I went crashing to the ground. Captain Cut-throat, who was just behind, tripped over me and collapsed in a tangle of skirts.

It was then that I heard a familiar voice . . .

'Take her! Don't let her escape!' yelled Thief-taker Craik.

Desperately I wriggled out from under Captain Cut-throat's huge bulk and rolled under a market stall parked at the side of the alley. I was just in time. The crowd pounced on Captain Cut-throat.

'Take her to the Eyrie,' said Craik coldly, and I heard Cut-throat gasp. 'We'll hang her at dawn and then stake her out on the rocks for the buzzards. Unless, that is, she is prepared to tell me where that weasel-faced viperfish vagabond Black-hearted Charlie is. He's the one I really want!'

I shrank back into the darkness under the stall, feeling terrible. As ruthless, despicable and downright bad as Captain Cut-throat was, I didn't want her to hang! And it was my clumsiness that had got her caught. Now she was being asked to squeal on a fellow pirate to save herself from the drop, but I knew that Captain Cut-throat would never give another pirate up. It went against all she stood for.

'Where's Black-hearted Charlie?' she mused. 'Mmm, now let me think . . .'

En Garde!

What?! I couldn't believe it! Surely, after all her lectures about honour amongst pirates, Captain Cut-throat wasn't going to hand me over to the hangman! I must have gasped in surprise, or maybe Captain Cut-throat *had* silently betrayed me, for the next minute the cover around the market stall was pulled back and I was staring straight into the face of Thief-taker Craik. It wasn't a pretty sight!

'Well, well, look what the cat threw up,' he said. 'A bonny little girl. But hold on, surely a girl could never be that ugly . . . Why, it's my old friend Black-hearted Charlie.' He prodded me with the tip of his sword. 'Out you come, boy.'

I rolled out from under the cart, and as I twisted, I drew the cutlass that was hidden amongst my skirts. I sprang to my feet, ready for battle.

'So, you're tired of life already, are you?' smirked the thief-taker, raising his own sword to the en garde position.

'No, I'm just tired of you,' I replied.

'Aaargh!' roared the thief-taker as he ran at me,

his sword raised above his head. He struck, but I parried as Sabre Sue had taught me, and the blow of his blade sent a judder right down to my feet. Soon the alley echoed to the clash and scrape of our swords as I fought for my life. I ducked as his blade zipped through the air and caught the wall of the alleyway with a clang and a fountain of sparks.

'Missed,' I cried, backing down the alleyway: a flight of steps behind me led down to the harbour below. Craik came again, chopping at the air like a frenzied butcher, his blade slicing a tear right across the skirt of my dress.

'Oi! That's my best frock!' I yelled, and charged back at him. Craik drew back his blade to strike, and as he thrust it forward, I quickly sidestepped and he went lumbering past me. The crowd surged forward, but I raised my sword and they quickly fell back again. All in the same movement, I spun round and whacked Craik square on the rump with the flat of my blade. He teetered forward, waving his arms like a windmill as he desperately tried to maintain his balance. But it was no good. With a cry he fell forward, clattering all the way down the steep flight of steps to the harbour.

As he sprawled, dazed and confused, on the cobbles below, I raced down the steps, leaped over him and charged towards the quay. The pirates

were already back on the *Betty Mae*, waving at me
to hurry up, so I dropped into an empty dinghy
and rowed away at top speed. As I climbed up the
rope ladder and onto the ship, Mop-head handed
me a telescope and pointed grimly back to Tortilla.
I looked through it and saw that the harbour
was deserted. Then she tilted the telescope and
I spotted a procession of soldiers and townsfolk
marching Captain Cut-Throat up the cliff path
from town. They were heading for a huge
stone jail set high above the port.

'That's Craik's Eyrie,' Kate told me. 'No
pirate who passes through its gates ever
comes out alive.'

I swallowed hard.
Because that was
where I knew
I'd have to go
next!

The Rescue

We've dropped anchor a couple of miles off shore and are waiting for nightfall, when I can mount my daring rescue attempt.

Why should I bother trying to save such a devious desperado, after the way she's treated me? Well, it *is* my fault that she's been captured. But more importantly, she has my precious phone tucked into her handbag, and I might really need that one day if I'm ever going to get home.

The pirates are very surprised that I wanted to go back for their boss. They think it's far too dangerous. As Rawcliffe Annie said, 'She's been a good cap'n, but deserting her is no less than she'd do to us. It's every girl for herself at a time like this!'

But I've finally got them to agree to at least give me until dawn before they sail away for ever. (In return for my share of all the spoils from Tortilla!)

Since then I've been repacking my explorer's rucksack. I'm taking everything with me – including the hunting knife and torch that mysteriously reappeared on my hammock last night! I'm also going to take a grappling hook on a length of rope, a spring-loaded mini harpoon gun, and the one remaining clockwork limpet. I've decided that the only way to get to the Eyrie unseen is to climb the massive cliff-face. The pirates think it's impossible, but I reckon that with all my tree-climbing in the jungle and in the rigging of the *Betty Mae* I have a good chance of making it.

And now, while I wait for the sun to go down, I'm writing this – which may well be my last ever journal entry! I'm happy that I've got it all up to date at last. But if the next page is blank, you'll know that Thief-taker Craik has finished my exploring days for ever!

aargh!

(Sorry missed a spread!)

A Hard Climb

As dusk smudged the cliffs above the
port, I lowered myself into the rowing
boat with Lizzie Hall. She pulled hard on
the oars with arms like steel cables, and
we were soon among the rocky outcrops
at the base of the huge cliffs on which
the Eyrie stood.

'Good luck, Charlie,' she whispered
as I jumped into the surf. 'Remember
we can't wait beyond dawn!'

I gave her a silent thumbs-up, then
waded up to the slime-covered rocks
and started to climb. It was very dark
now and I had to feel for every hand-
and foothold, my nose just inches from
the spray-spattered cliff-face, the waves
crashing around my ankles as they broke
against the shore.

Gradually I left the sea far
below. The roar of the wind
replaced the roar of the
waves, and tried its

146

best to pluck me from the side of the cliff. I
held on for dear life, flattening myself against
the rock, my fingers aching with the effort of
holding on.

A Helping Hand

Finally I hauled myself onto a small outcrop
and discovered a cluster of buzzards' nests. I was
surprised to find so many packed onto the ledge,
but then I realized they probably fed off the
bodies of the pirates that Craik staked out on the
rocks. Ugh! Tomorrow that could be me!

I lay against one of the nests to catch my
breath and realized almost
straight away that this
was a very bad idea.
There were two
chicks in the nest,
ugly things covered
in scraps of feather and down,
with nasty hooked beaks – and
they were nearly as big as me!
How big must their mother be?

I wondered as the chicks screamed and lunged at me. Then *WHAM!* the mother's feet slammed into my back, knocking me forward. Her talons closed tight around the collar of my coat, and I was lifted up into the inky darkness.

I didn't know if I was above sea or land. The wind rushed past at an alarming speed, so I grabbed the buzzard tight round her ankles in case she suddenly decided to drop me. Then the moon came out from behind a thick cloud, and I could see that we were racing along the cliff top towards the Eyrie. We were heading exactly where I wanted to go, but I knew the buzzard might change course at any moment. I had to do something before she headed out over the water. But what?

Then I had an idea – I'd drop anchor!

Hanging on desperately to the buzzard's scaly leg with one hand, I managed to reach round and loosen the flap of my rucksack. Scrabbling around inside, I found the grappling hook.

Somehow I managed to tie its rope around my belt. Then I let the hook fall away through the dark to the ground below.

I heard it skim and bounce across the coarse

grasses of the cliff top, then *THUMP!* it caught on a rock and the rope was pulled rigid. I held on as tight as I could to the buzzard's legs as we came to a sudden, bone-juddering halt in mid-air. Then the startled buzzard started to plummet towards the ground.

She released her grip on my coat and flapped her broad wings desperately, slowing our fall, but she couldn't go forward while I clung stubbornly to her ankles. Then, just before we crashed onto the cliff top, I let the buzzard go and she soared back up into the sky.

I hit the ground hard but managed to break my fall by rolling in a way I'd learned from the gorillas back in my days in the jungle. Then I lay on the rough grass until I got my breath back, peering into the darkness.

A couple of hundred metres along the cliff top, the forbidding silhouette of the Eyrie rose black against the milky, moonlit clouds that were racing across the sky. I picked up the grappling hook, wound the rope around my arm and crept towards it.

Into The Eyrie

The Eyrie towered high above me; the cliffs on which it stood dropping out of sight below. I crouched in the shadows at the base of the huge stone walls and checked around for guards.

Then I took out the mini harpoon and jammed the shaft of the grappling hook into its barrel. Cranking back the spring loader, I shouldered the harpoon gun, aimed it at the top of the wall and fired.

I launched the grappling hook over the wall.

BOOF! The grappling hook shot high into the night sky, the rope snaking out behind. It curved over the top of the wall and I heard the clang as it clattered against the other side. I waited to see if the noise had alerted any guards, and then pulled on the rope until the grappling hook caught fast. Then I scrambled up the rope, over the top and onto a shadowy walkway.

I studied the layout of the fortress. Below

lay a courtyard. One end was bordered by a guardhouse. I could see the guards' silhouettes in the windows, slapping each other on the back and raising tankards to their lips. At the other end was the cellblock, so full of tiny barred windows that it looked like a honeycomb. Captain Cut-throat would be somewhere in there. Apart from a sleepy-looking guard at each of the corner turrets, the rest of the castle seemed deserted.

I darted along the walkway on top of the wall, creeping past a guarded turret, until I came to a door that I hoped would lead me down to the cellblock. The door, of course, was locked, so I pulled out the poison dart from my rucksack and inserted it into the large keyhole. All my practising had been worth it, for after a moment of fiddling and scraping I heard a clunk and the door pushed open.

A stairway led down inside the wide wall. It

I picked the lock with the fish's dart.

was inky black and I had to feel my way down, counting the steps to get an idea of how far I was descending. I counted 267 before I came to another door. I must have descended about half-way down from the top of the huge external wall and guessed I would now be on a level with the cells. The door had a grille, and I looked through onto a corridor, lit by a torch burning on the opposite wall. I picked this lock, slid into the corridor and crept along the wall in the direction of the cellblock.

Breakout!

The corridor led onto a landing extending all the way round the cellblock. The cells were built around a central well that was open from floor to ceiling, and leaning over, I could see at least twenty more landings disappearing into the gloom below me. Each landing contained over a hundred cells! How on earth was I going to find Captain Cut-throat amongst that lot?

But my luck seemed to be holding, because as I leaned against the wall wondering what to do next,

I heard a familiar voice singing from somewhere on the landing below.

'*We were poor little wives of black-hearted pirates, who left us at home, playing at mum . . .*' It was the captain.

'Quiet in there!' yelled the night turnkey as he patrolled the floor below, his feet scraping along the landing. He banged on Captain Cut-throat's cell door. 'Did you hear me? I said, *Shut yer trap*,' and he shuffled off down a flight of steps to continue his rounds.

I crept down the stone steps, along to Captain Cut-throat's cell, and tapped on the door.

'Captain, it's me. Charlie Small.'

'Charlie, my boy,' she cried, hurrying over to the bars set in the door. 'I knew you'd come. I knew you wouldn't let me swing.'

'I owe you one,' I whispered back. 'For saving me from that octopus.'

I studied the lock on her cell door and realized straight away that it was much more complicated than those I had already opened. There was no way that I could pick it, so I took the clockwork limpet out of my rucksack and clamped it over the huge lock mechanism.

With the limpet fully wound, I flicked the switch and the diamond-coated blades started to spin and cut into the heavy oak door. At first the muffled humming noise wasn't too bad, but when the blades hit the ironwork of the lock, a high-pitched whine cut through the stillness of the night. I jammed my rucksack over the limpet, trying to lessen the noise, but the damage was already done.

'Who's making that noise?' demanded the turnkey from a few landings below. 'Stop it, I say. You'll wake the whole place.' I heard the scuffing of his feet as he made his way along the landing and started to climb the stairs.

What's that noise?

The Turnkey

The blades squealed as they ate through the lock, sending shards of metal curling onto the floor. I willed the limpet to speed up. I willed the turnkey to slow down!

As the old jailer shuffled onto our landing, the limpet blades were already through the door and spinning silently in the cell. I yanked the limpet off and heaved at the large cut circle of wood and metal in the door; they clattered to the ground. The door swung open and Captain Cut-throat stepped out onto the landing.

'Let's go,' she said, and I led her back up the way I had come.

'Stop!' cried the old turnkey from behind us. 'Stop or I'll shoot!'

PATANG!

A bullet ricocheted off of the steps as we disappeared onto the landing above.

'Catch us if you can, old man,' cried Captain Cut-throat, and a piercing whistle filled the cellblock as the turnkey tried to rouse the guards.

We Take Flight

Along the corridor we raced, puffing up the 267 steps and out onto the walkway on top of the wall. Now we could hear the sound of running feet, of voices calling and shouting. The next minute fifty fearsome guards armed with pikes were piling out of a doorway on the opposite walkway. The guards on the turrets were hurriedly priming their muskets. There was no way we could shin down the rope that still snaked to the cliff top below. We would be sitting ducks.

The guards charged, and I thought we'd had it, but then Captain Cut-throat reached inside her blouse, drawing out a brace of pistols.

'They didn't look in there when they frisked me.' She winked. I couldn't say I blamed them! She fired in the air and the guards stopped in mid-charge, ducking down in the shadows. Then the musket-men on the turrets fired back at us and lead shot went whistling over our heads.

'Give up while you still can!' shouted the chief guard, and a dozen pikes came sailing towards us, clattering onto the walkway around our feet. Captain Cut-throat fired again and I heard her bullet ping off the chief guard's helmet. Then I had an idea.

'Keep them at bay,' I said as I opened my rucksack and unfolded the giant leaf I had kept from my days in the jungle. I laid one of the pikes across its width and hacked the pole to the correct length with my hunting knife. I did the same with another pike for the length of the leaf, and then, using the string I kept in my explorer's kit, quickly bound the two poles together to make a cross. All the time Captain Cut-throat was firing and loading her pistols as fast as she could. The guards were gradually moving closer, while those on the turrets were busy firing and reloading their muskets. Luckily for us they were lousy shots!

'Whatever you're doing, hurry up,' cried the captain.

String

Giant leaf

Pike Poles

'They'll be on us in a minute.' I cut four slots into the leathery leaf and poked the ends of the poles through them.

'Do you trust me?' I asked the captain as I stepped between two of the outer wall's crenellations.

'With my life, Charlie, with my life.'

That's good, I thought, because that's just what you're about to do. I stood my contraption on its end, grabbed the cross-pole and shouted to the captain. 'Hold on around my waist. Quick!'

The captain let off one more shot and grabbed me around my middle.

'Geronimo!' I yelled and we jumped out into the black night.

Captain Cut-throat was heavy and we dropped like a stone as pikes whizzed over our heads and bullets peppered holes in the leaf! It was all I could do to hold onto my homemade kite as it flapped wildly above us.

'Do something, Charlie!' cried the captain.

I fought against the power of the rushing wind and levelled the kite. Immediately we caught an up-draught, the leaf filled with air and then we were gliding out over the cliff top

as the sky flooded yellow with the rising sun.

We'd better hurry, I thought, or the *Betty Mae* will leave us behind. I tipped the kite and we swooped across the golden water towards the ship.

Captain Cut-throat slipped from my waist and grabbed me round my knees. 'Hurry up, Charlie. I'm slipping!'

Back on Board The 'Betty Mae'

We drifted lower and lower as we got closer to the *Betty Mae*. Soon Captain Cut-throat was running along the top of the waves, holding onto my trainers for dear life! And the *Betty Mae* was on the move! We called to them. We yelled and we hollered!

'Over here, you numbskulls,' bellowed the captain as we swooped in like a drunken albatross. 'Don't you recognize an order when you— *Glug, glug, glug.*' The captain's yells were cut short as she slowly disappeared under the waves. Then I hit the water, too, and the kite collapsed on top of us. We clung to the floating leaf until Lizzie rowed out to pick us up.

Now we're coursing through the waves at top speed, the sun ahead of us, an action-packed night behind. But we're not out of trouble yet. Not far behind us, and going like the clappers, is Craik in a galleon bristling with guns. It won't be long before he's upon us again and I have to fight for my life. My little barrel-boat is hidden down here in my cabin, waiting for a clear chance to escape, but now is *definitely* not the right time to use it – I'd be a sitting duck! I know I'll have to go back on deck soon and prepare to fight, but without any of Jakeman's special inventions I don't know what chance we'll have. Craik's ship has more cannon than ours, and the *Betty Mae* still hasn't been repaired from our last battle.

Oh well, at least things can't get any worse. Can they . . . ?

Unexpected Visitors

'*Ship ahoy!*' called Rawcliffe Annie from up in the rigging.

'We know that, you blithering idiot!' yelled Cut-throat. 'Craik's been on our tail since sunrise.'

'No, *another* ship ahoy!' cried Annie, pointing off our starboard side.

I rushed over, peered through my telescope and knew things had just got a lot, *lot* worse! Hurtling towards us was a phantom boat as white as ivory, the morning sun tinting her sails yellow. Her bows were carved into the mask of a grinning skull, whose eyes were windows that glowed dull red from lanterns swinging inside. On deck stood her crew, also dressed in white.

The phantom boat as it hurtled towards us

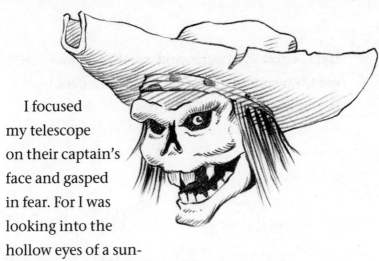

I focused my telescope on their captain's face and gasped in fear. For I was looking into the hollow eyes of a sun-bleached, bone-white skull! The ivory ship was crewed by skeletons!

'Friend or foe?' asked Captain Cut-throat.

I didn't say a word; I just handed her my telescope.

'Foe!' she replied, without even looking. 'I've just remembered – we don't have any friends! *Man the cannon and sharpen your cutlasses!*' she roared. '*And prepare to dance the Waltz of Death!*'

The Waltz of Death

Captain Cut-throat turned the *Betty Mae* in a wide sweeping curve away from the other galleons and then doubled back, straight towards Craik's ship. Craik had turned to follow the phantom ship, which was following us, and we were now all sailing in a circle in the famous Waltz of Death. Each ship had its cannons trained on the other two. If one fired, the other two would direct all their fire at the attacker. So it was a stalemate. No one dared shoot first!

Round and round and round we sailed as the sun rose high into the sky. The sea had become very calm and not even the cry of a seagull disturbed the silence, only the creaking of the rigging and the occasional crack of wind in a sail. Slowly we all came to a standstill in a classic face-off. Would anybody fire first?

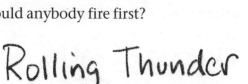

The Waltz

← ships →

of death!

Rolling Thunder

The seconds grew into long, silent minutes until the tension became unbearable.

Then Craik's cannons erupted into life and I had to dive for cover.

'Let 'em have it!' hollered the Captain Cut-throat in return. 'Fire at will!'

Our cannons roared in answer and were joined by those of the ivory galleon. The air was filled with a terrifying thunderous sound and great billows of smoke rolled across the surface of the sea until we could see nothing at all.

When the cannons finally fell silent and the smoke cleared, all that remained of Craik's ship was a mass of floating driftwood. Sailors were clinging to the wreckage and clambering into the lifeboats. Craik himself was straddling a length of broken mast; he was screaming at us and shaking his fist. We'd beaten him again!

'Brilliant!' I cried. 'It's all over!'

'Not quite, sonny,' said Cut-throat. 'Look!' And she pointed towards the other great galleon, which was heading straight for us like some terrible ghostly apparition. Her skeletal captain stood at the bows, pistol at the ready.

'Who are they?' I asked, my heart beating fast.

'The ghosts of dirty, stinking pirates, I'll be bound,' replied Captain Cut-throat. 'Best say your prayers, boy.'

The Final Battle

The approaching galleon looked like a huge, sinister wedding cake, decorated from top to bottom with intricate carvings of decapitated heads and skulls. She fired, and the *Betty Mae*'s cannons spat back.

Splinters of wood whipped through the air all around us. Smoke filled our lungs and stung our eyes as we stumbled around the deck. I was in the middle of a major battle and it was complete confusion. But there was no time to be scared: I was too busy carrying out Cut-throat's orders – trimming the sails and hauling on ropes – while the pirates fired shot after shot from the gun deck.

Gradually we manoeuvred the *Betty Mae* alongside the foe. 'Prepare to board!' yelled Captain Cut-throat. 'Take no prisoners!'

But as I grabbed my cutlass and prepared to fight for my life, a horde of ghost pirates came swinging through the smoke, their cutlasses singing in the air. They dropped onto the deck of the *Betty Mae*, led by the ferocious skeleton warrior. A mass of wild hair sprouted from beneath his hat, his skull grinned and his hollow eyes stared. He raised his sword, ready to slice Captain Cut-throat in two.

And then he stopped!

Ivy?

'Ivy?' he gasped, and pulled and pulled at his face until it came off in his hand . . .

It was a mask – a skull mask – and underneath was a rather ordinary-looking man.

'Ted?' she replied, and they fell into each other's arms. It was Captain Cut-throat's husband and his gang.

Soon all the pirates were hugging, their old quarrels forgotten, and I'd never been so relieved in my life!

'Tonight we'll have a party to end all parties,' roared Ted – or Captain Bones, as he preferred to be called. 'You're all invited aboard the

Saracen's Skull at eight o'clock sharp. Bring a barrel!'

Now, as the pirates sit around chatting and laughing, I've crept off to my room to write up these latest adventures and to check on my barrel-boat before I finally make my escape.

Yes, I'm finally going to do it! Tonight, during the party, I'm determined to slip away. Even if I have to pedal for days! I've had enough of pirates and thief-takers and I want to go home!

My Escape From The 'Betty Mae'

I've done it! I've escaped and I'm floating through the sky by the strangest means of transport ever! It's a bit hard to write dangling like this, but I can't wait any longer to explain what happened . . .

I waited until the party was in full swing on the *Saracen's Skull*. Then, as the pirates sang their bawdy sea shanties and danced the hornpipe, I crept back aboard the *Betty Mae*. Heart beating fast, I sneaked into the captain's empty cabin and, by the light of my torch, found the dress she had worn on the raid, still damp from her ducking in the sea. Hung with it was the little matching handbag and I snapped open the clasp and felt inside. There they were, my mobile and the wind-up charger! I pocketed them and scuttled back out of the door and down to my room. Here I uncovered my barrel-boat and then, rather awkwardly, dragged it along the deserted corridors and up the steep wooden steps that led onto the main deck.

The noise from the party on the *Saracen's Skull* covered the splash as I dropped my barrel-boat over the *Betty Mae*'s side. With my rucksack on my back, packed with all my explorer's stuff, a slab of smoked whale blubber for the journey and a large bag of gold, I climbed down the rope ladder into the floating barrel.

Whoa! It sank *very* low in the water, and only my head and shoulders showed above the waves. I found the pedals with my feet and, crossing my fingers that the contraption would work, pushed against them with all my might. Slowly they started to turn and the paddles inched the barrel forwards. Then, as I built up speed, they began to turn with ease: the paddles churned the water and I stuttered away from the ship. It worked!

So long, suckers, I thought. But I hadn't gone more than a hundred metres when I was spotted. It was Bobo, of course.

'Deserter!' she screamed from the rigging, bringing the pirates swarming to the ship's rails.

'Traitor!' shouted Captain Cut-throat.

'Come back, you dog!' growled her husband. 'I'll skin you alive.'

Go back? No fear! I paddled as fast as I could, but was soon under attack. A musket ball struck the barrel a glancing blow and water started to seep through the cracked side.

I started to sink.

'Help!' I cried.

'So long, shrimp!' the pirates shouted. 'Say hello to Davy Jones's locker!'

And while Bobo screamed with delight, they went back to their celebrations.

But I didn't sink. Not quite, anyway.

As my barrel-boat broke up in the water, I managed to grab a couple of boards and wedge them through the netting containing the coconuts. By lying flat across the boards and kicking my legs, I managed to doggy-paddle through the waves and away into the night.

A New World

It was a cold, lonely night, and I shivered as I paddled onwards. I had no idea which direction to go, so I just let the currents take me where they would. I had left the pirates and Thief-taker Craik far behind and that was good enough for me. Then, when the sun finally rose, I found myself completely alone on a wide, flat sea. But it looked nothing like the one I had sailed on in the *Betty Mae*. The green-grey sea had been replaced by one that shone as bright as silver, and columns of rock

dotted the seascape – home to flocks of albino
cormorants that watched me like silent ghosts.

The sea was perfectly still, and I floated
through the crags and rocks for hour after hour,

The Albino Cormorants

amazed by the weirdness of the place, and only slowly realizing that my tiny raft was sinking lower and lower in the water.

The wooden planks had become waterlogged and I had to get rid of some weight, or I would be dragged down to the bottom of the ocean.

I opened my rucksack and reached inside for the heaviest thing – the fat bag of gold I'd brought from the pirates' ship. 'Goodbye, life of riches,' I sighed as I upended the bag and watched every last doubloon disappear below the waves.

'Do you mind?' snapped a strange little ball of a fish, breaking the surface of the waves. 'You very nearly hit me.'

The Puffer Fish Balloon

'I'm sorry,' I gasped, surprised to find myself talking to a fish.

'Well, you should be more careful where you dump your rubbish,' he said, all puffed up.

'I said I'm sorry,' I barked. 'Who are you anyway, telling people what to do?'

'Who am I?' gasped the fish, gulping in a

mouthful of air, doubling in size and bouncing on the surface of the sea. 'Who am I? Why, I'm the famous purple puffer fish.'

'Famous for what? I've never heard of you.'

'Famous for holding my breath,' boasted the puffer fish. 'I am world champion, the best breath-holder in the known universe, the emperor of arrested exhalation, the . . .'

But I had stopped listening to the puffer fish's bragging: an idea started to form in my mind.

'Bet I can hold my breath longer than you,' I said, reaching inside my rucksack for the ball of string.

'I doubt that,' bragged the puffer fish. 'I can hold my breath for over a year.'

'I don't believe you,' I said.

'Just watch me, then,' said the puffer fish. He sucked in such a huge gulp of air that he blew up to the size of a garden shed and started to float up into the sky.

I quickly threw two loops of string over his spiked back and tied them to my sinking platform.

Slowly the puffer fish lifted us out of the waves.

That was hours ago, and we're still going up. I can see for miles in every direction, but there's no sign of land. I'm sure this strange puffer fish can't really hold his breath for a year, but it looks like I might be flying for a while, so I'm going to tie myself to the plank and try to get some sleep.

I'll write again when we land.

What Goes Up...

Everything has changed again! I'm now sheltering behind a large rock on an almost featureless ice-field, the wind whipping up tiny shards to sting my face.

The puffer fish and I drifted across that vast ocean for months and months, the scenery never ending and never changing. I lived on coconuts, whale blubber, rainwater, seaweed, and raw eggs that I managed to pinch from the cormorant nests as we drifted by. As the puffer fish was too busy holding his breath to hold a conversation, it was a very lonely trip. The most I ever got out of him was the occasional squeak of 'Yes' or 'No'.

On the dawning of the three hundred and sixty-fifth day, however, I woke to a completely different scene. At some time during the night we had left the ocean far behind and were now sailing above a patchwork of fields and hills, farmsteads and hamlets. Happily I waved at the people below. But when they saw me, they started to shout and wave me away.

'What's wrong?' I called, but we were too high to hear their reply, and anyway I had no way of changing the direction of the puffer-fish balloon. So we sailed on until the hills grew larger, the air became colder and the sky greyer. Soon we were floating above the icy tops of jiggedy-jaggedy mountains.

I leaned down and snapped off a large ice stalagmite and licked it like a huge ice-pop. It tasted delicious and mysterious, like a wish or a dream, better than any lolly I had ever tried. I snapped off another, then another. I couldn't get enough! But soon I began to feel drowsy and my

I couldn't get enough of these icicle lollys!

eyelids grew heavy. As I drifted off to sleep, I heard the puffer fish squeak, splutter and, with a huge raspberry, collapse like a punctured party balloon.

'World record!' I heard him shout as we ricocheted across the mountain range and zoomed at a thousand miles an hour into a billowing, blinding snowstorm. But by then, I was sleeping like a baby . . .

Publisher's note:
This is where the second diary ends.
Keep your eyes peeled for more stories
from Charlie Small!

A Pirate Dictionary

Here are the meanings of some pirate words:

Blackjack – Another word for the Jolly Roger.

Booty – Stuff stolen from enemy ships.

Bounty – A reward offered for the capture of a pirate.

Broadside – To fire all the cannons on one side of a ship at the same time.

Cabin Boy – The ship's servant.

Cat O'Nine Tails – A terrible whip with nine knotted strings – Ouch!

Cut-throat – A particularly vicious pirate.

Doldrums – An area near the equator, where there is virtually no wind for sailing ships.

First Mate – Second in command to the captain.

Grappling Iron – A tool with three hooks used to hold an enemy ship close enough to board.

Hardtack – A very hard biscuit!

Keelhaul – To punish someone by dragging them under the keel of a ship.

Landlubber – A poor sailor.

Loot – To rob!

Merchantman – A trade ship.

JAKEMAN

We invite the public's inspection of our world famous products, engineered to the highest standard and for every possible event.

Come and see our marvellous machines!

FLYING MACHINES: for the intrepid airborne adventurer, powered entirely by elastic energy and good for a thousand miles.

◆

SUBMARINAMALS: shaped like a range of underwater creatures, from clockwork seahorses for net repairs to hydro-electric whales that can sleep a crew of three hundred and stay submerged for up to ten years.

◆

THE MOLE: A remarkable tunnel-digging machine, incorporating strong paddle arms and a spiral snout. On-board kitchen facilities and bunk bed optional. A must for civil engineers and underground explorers alike.

S WORKS LTD

Many more inventions available, including compost-powered rockets, radio-controlled shoes, steam-powered rhinos, and much, much more.

Visit our works at your earliest convenience.

My Top Ten ~~Super~~ Heroes.

1) Spiderman

2) ~~Batman~~ Dr. Who.

3) Sherlock Holmes.

4) Tintin.

5) Batman.

6) Dan Dare (in my dad's old comics).

7) Robin Hood.

8) Dr. Syn The Scarecrow (from my Grandad's old books).

9) Zorro.

10) Superman.   I like Tarzan too!

Some of my favourite explorers and adventurers (in no particular order)

Neil Armstrong and Buzz Aldrin (1st men on the moon)

Scott and Amundsen (explorers of the Antarctic)

Dr. Livingstone (I presume) and Stanley.

Ranulph Fiennes

Hillary and Tensing (1st to climb everest - with kendal mint cake?)

Jacques Cousteau (underwater explorer and inventor of the aqualung.)

Yuri Gagarin - 1st man in space

Ernest Shackleton.

Capt Cook.

Mary Kingsley (Victorian explorer of remote and dangerous parts of Africa).

My wish List

Things I wish I'd packed in my explorer's kit:

1) More food, especially chocolate.

2) ~~Most~~ ~~Mosque~~ Mossy spray.

3) Change of underwear.

4) My gameboy.

5) An explorer's hand book.

6) ~~Compass~~ (got one off the skeletal explorer.)